Thomas was enthralled

But something was different ⋯⋯⋯⋯⋯⋯⋯⋯⋯
they'd met. No longer was the ⋯⋯⋯⋯⋯⋯⋯⋯⋯
face or a confidence in her stance as once had been. Instead,
he saw a wariness in her eyes, a brave tilt to her proud chin,
and a challenged air to the way she stood, as if she were
readying herself for an assault.

Even so, she was magnificent to fix one's eyes upon. Her
presence seemed to outshine all other ladies around her.
Under any other circumstances, Thomas would have had no
reluctance about rushing up to reacquaint himself with her,
perhaps even pursue her, for she was exactly what he wished
for in a wife and more.

But Lady Katherine Montbatten could not be his—would
probably laugh in his face if he even suggested a match
between them. No. She probably hated the very mention of
the Thornton name. And he didn't blame her.

Katherine had almost been his sister-in-law.

KIMBERLEY COMEAUX is a pastor's wife who wears many hats, including choir director, women's ministries leader, and Web designer for her church. Her first love, however, remains dreaming up and writing inspirational romances for the wonderful Heartsong readers! She lives in Cajun Louisiana with her husband, Brian; teenage son, Tyler; and their two dogs.

Books by Kimberley Comeaux

HEARTSONG PRESENTS
HP296—One More Chance
HP351—Courtin' Patience
HP400—Susannah's Secret
HP472—The Sheriff and the Outlaw
HP552—The Vicar's Daughter

The Engagement

Kimberley Comeaux

Heartsong Presents

To Sandee Luke, Carrie Levron, and Debbie Triggs, good friends and Tuesday night coffee buddies. Thank you all for listening with patience as I ramble on about plots and English accents.

A note from the Author:
I love to hear from my readers! You may correspond with me by writing:

Kimberley Comeaux
Author Relations
PO Box 719
Uhrichsville, OH 44683

ISBN 1-59310-125-2

THE ENGAGEMENT

Our mission is to publish and distribute inspirational products offering exceptional value and biblical encouragement to the masses.

All Scripture quotations are taken from the King James Version of the Bible.

All of the characters and events in this book are fictitious. Any resemblance to actual persons, living or dead, or to actual events is purely coincidental.

PRINTED IN THE U.S.A.

Or check out our Web site at www.heartsongpresents.com

one

London, England—Spring 1814

"Is it just I, or do you find these dinner parties dreadfully dull?"

"I, too, share the sentiment, but then again, I find many things dull. You, on the other hand, have a better excuse than I," Trevor Kent, the Duke of Northingshire, answered his friend as they watched the guests who were in attendance at the Beckinghams' party. "I don't imagine you can compare adventure on the high seas and your escapade with pirates with our monotonous English society and their dreary little efforts at entertainment."

Lord Thomas Thornton gave North, as the duke was known to his friends, a sardonic grin. "You could not be further from the truth. I didn't like dinner parties before my 'adventure,' as you call it, and I will die a happy man if I never get on another boat," he informed him. "And it was a merchant ship that rescued me, by the by."

"Yes, but let's keep that between us, eh? The story sounds so much more thrilling to add the pirates."

Thomas chuckled. "If it had been pirates, I might have been the dead man everyone thought I was!"

Thomas and North shared a sobering glance. "Indeed. God must surely smile on all the Thorntons, since both you and your brother have truly been blessed this past year."

While Thomas could now make light of his harrowing scrape with death, it had been the blackest time of his life. When he was a lieutenant in the Royal Navy, his ship had been destroyed during a horrendous storm at sea. He and only a handful of others managed to survive by holding on to pieces of the hull until a merchant ship heading to Canada picked them up. Because of the war between the Britons of Canada and the United States, he was not able to return home until nearly a year later. Unfortunately, during this time, all aboard the ship had been declared dead. And that is what his family and friends had been told.

His surprising homecoming was made bittersweet when he learned his young wife, with whom he'd had an arranged marriage, had died giving birth to their son, Tyler. His brother, Nicholas, had looked after the baby until Thomas could return.

"If only He would also bless me with a wife as He bestowed upon my dear brother." Thomas smiled as he referred to his new sister-in-law, Christina, who was also the vicar's daughter in his hometown of Malbury. That smile dimmed a little as he recalled his past. "Dear Anne, my late wife, was a good woman and gave me a wonderful son. Perhaps I have no right to want more."

"Of course you have a right. Which is why you have dragged me to this 'dreadfully dull' affair, or have you forgotten? We must endure such events to find you a wife and a mother for young Tyler," North stated matter-of-factly. "Now tell me which young miss has caught your eye, and I'll see to the introduction."

Thomas made a show of scanning the room. "Therein, unfortunately, lies my problem. They are all very nice and most comely to admire, but. . ." His voice drifted off, as he was unable to put his feelings to words.

"Mmm." North nodded. "I know what you mean. You are searching for what I've sought after for quite some time—someone who is original."

"Exactly!"

"Someone who is pretty yet doesn't give the impression of being like all the rest."

"Yes!"

"She must be easy to talk to and not bore you with relentless chattering about fashions or gossip about the neighbors," North added to the list.

"Absolutely!"

"And above all, she must be loyal, loving, and kind!"

"Here, here!"

They held a moment of silence as they both paused to think about what they had just said. Suddenly, they glanced at each other and began to laugh.

"I believe I just described my dog," North sputtered between laughs.

Thomas wiped the moisture from his eyes. "I was thinking of my horse!"

It took a few moments for both men to regain control. By then the whole room was staring at them with curiosity and censure, the latter, of course, from the older set.

"I believe we have drawn enough attention to ourselves this evening. Perhaps we should say our good-byes to our host."

Thomas nodded. "Indeed. I do not think I shall find my bride among this crowd, anyway. Perhaps I should take a page from my brother and start attending services in various churches across the shire. There could be another vicar's daughter like my brother's wife, out there—somewhere."

North grinned. "Or you could forgo your loathing of sea travel and go with me back to America. My cousin and I have established a sugar plantation near the city of New Orleans. I was supposed to go and see how he was faring this last year, but a war was still going on. Now that it seems to be over, I shall leave in just a few months."

"I think I've seen enough of North America. We were docked in some little Canadian harbor for two months, and I was glad to leave," Thomas answered with a shudder. "If I cannot find a bride on English soil, then I shall remain a single man."

"Well, if you. . ." North's sentence drifted to a halt when they both noticed the room had become quiet. They glimpsed around to see that all eyes had turned toward the door.

The woman who stood at the entrance to the hall was even more beautiful than the last time Thomas had seen her. Her light blond hair curled artfully about her face while the length of it was pinned atop her head and cascaded in tiny curls down the back. Even from where he stood, he could see the smoothness of her cheeks, the arch of her light brows, and the glow from her incredible golden eyes. Her dress was the color of bright copper, with delicate beaded lace at her neck and high waistline.

But something was different about her from the last time they'd met. No longer was there an enchanting smile on her face or a confidence in her stance as once had been. Instead, he saw a wariness in her eyes, a brave tilt to her proud chin, and a challenged air to the way she stood, as if she were readying herself for an assault.

Even so, she was magnificent to fix one's eyes upon. Her presence seemed to outshine all other ladies around her. Under any other circumstances, Thomas would have had no reluctance about rushing up to reacquaint himself with her, perhaps even pursue her, for she was exactly what he wished for in a wife and more.

But Lady Katherine Montbatten could not be his—would probably laugh in his face if he even suggested a match between them. No. She probably hated the very mention of the Thornton name. And he didn't blame her.

Katherine had almost been his sister-in-law.

When his brother, Nicholas, the Earl of Kenswick, returned from the war, he'd been wounded and bitter from all he'd seen and done during the battles. In his confused and anxious state, he'd broken his betrothal with Katherine just months before the wedding and conducted himself in a manner in which no gentleman of his station should behave. During this time, their father had died, then Nicholas had thought Thomas was lost to him, also. With the help of Christina, the vicar's daughter, he'd come to realize he needed God's help and forgiveness. Since then, he'd completely changed and settled down to family life at Kenswick Hall with his new bride.

But that didn't change the fact that Katherine had been hurt by the whole affair.

As the crowd around them started to move about and resume their chatter, he watched her trying to smile while greeting their hosts for the party, Lord and Lady Beckingham. She tried to pretend nothing was wrong, but clearly something was.

And Thomas had a horrible feeling he knew the reason. "She has been ostracized by the *ton*," he murmured, hoping he was not correct in his summation, for the *ton* represented England's noble families and was known to judge harshly, even among their own relations.

"Not entirely," North corrected. "Only by the marriageable bachelors of the *ton*. Of course, there are always those who would have other propositions for her, but it is good she has her family to support her."

Thomas grimaced. "Does Nicholas know?"

North nodded. "He does and has repeatedly offered to make amends by providing her father money to add to her dowry, but he was refused." He sighed. "The Montbattens are nearly as rich as your family, so, of course, money is not the problem."

Thomas once again studied her brave features as she pasted on a smile and greeted those around her. "Why the censure? Others have suffered a broken engagement with little repercussions."

"Apparently some idiot started a rumor after Katherine declined his offer to dance at a ball. From there, the lie grew bigger, and before it was all done, it sounded as if your brother had engaged in a duel because he'd found Katherine in a compromising situation with another man—though far from the truth." He shook his head distastefully as he referred to the duels Thomas's brother had fought after he returned from the war; they'd had nothing actually to do with Katherine.

They were quiet for a moment, both watching her from where they stood at the back of the room. "She is beautiful," Thomas murmured, voicing his thoughts.

"Beautiful but cold," the duke stated bluntly. "She was always aware of her beauty, Thomas, and in my opinion over-confident in the fact that many adored her. I always knew she wasn't the one for your brother. I'm just sorry he ended it so badly."

Thomas knew all this, since he'd been acquainted with her before he was married. But he'd always felt that her coolness was a façade, almost as if she were afraid to show who she really was. He would see flashes of wit and intelligence before they were quickly banked beneath a serene smile and cultured conversation.

"It would seem her confidence has taken quite a blow," he finally commented.

North shrugged. "I would not doubt it." He tugged at his lapel. "Well, I've had enough of this scene. Would you like to leave now?"

"I believe I have changed my mind after all," he answered, his eyes still on Katherine.

His friend was silent for a moment, and when Thomas looked at him, he saw speculation and a little worry in his eyes. Thomas knew North wanted to say something more, but he only nodded and responded, "I will fetch us more punch then."

He barely noticed North's departure, for he was already scanning the crowd once more for the beautiful blond.

He was stunned to find her golden eyes had found him first. Several unreadable emotions passed over her face as she gazed at him. Thomas was sure her next movement would be to jerk her eyes away from him in disgust once she realized who he was.

But she didn't.

Suddenly she smiled at him, and the confusing emotions that had been swirling in her eyes were gone. Thomas felt the smile all the way down to the pit of his stomach and did not take one breath, so stunned was he by her reaction.

Thomas was afraid to think of how he felt as she began to make her way to him. He didn't dare speculate on what this could mean. He refused to have expectations.

Yet. . .he could not help but hope.

❧

All afternoon, Lady Katherine Montbatten, the eldest daughter of the Duke of Ravenhurst, had meticulously plotted her revenge. With help and much coaching from her cousin Theodora, they derived the perfect way to execute their plan— the plan that would vindicate both her and her family and teach the Thorntons a much-needed lesson.

Of course, Katherine had initial doubts about using Nicholas Thornton's brother, Thomas, to do the deed, but Theodora convinced her Thomas must have had a hand in persuading

Nicholas to break their engagement. And, besides, what was done to her reputation hurt not only her but also her parents and her siblings. It was only fair the whole Thornton clan suffer as well.

For over a year, Katherine had had to endure humiliation after humiliation as more rumors and speculation spread about her. Slowly, she noticed the offers for her hand had been rescinded and her admirers had fallen away. Even her brother, Cameron, had striven to correct the false assumptions about her character, but he'd been unable to do much good.

The horrible rumors would not die, and she was ruined for it.

And then Theodora had told her about Thomas Thornton returning to society and finding out his wife had died in childbirth. As a widower, she pointed out, he would soon be in need of a wife.

From there they plotted and schemed on the steps they should take. Even though Katherine doubted and wanted to give up the whole plan, Theodora was there cheering her on, telling her she would feel so much better once revenge was theirs.

Now as they stood on the threshold of Beckingham Hall, she once again was plagued with doubts. A part of her still knew what she was about to do was wrong. It was the same part that spoke to her through Sunday sermons from the vicar and nagged at her when she tried to read her Bible. The last time she'd opened her Bible, the Scripture in Romans leaped out at her: "Vengeance is mine; I will repay, saith the Lord." But Theodora had convinced her that, in this instance, God surely understood.

And to make sure she had no more doubts on that score, Katherine had put away her Bible and refused to bring it out until all of this was over.

She wasn't sure God understood at all; otherwise, why would she be plagued with so much guilt?

But tonight there was no going back. They had arrived, and already she had noticed that, indeed, Thomas was in attendance at the party.

She was just not prepared for the effect his presence would have on her. She was certainly not prepared for the memories of how fond she had been of him or how truly nice he'd been during her engagement to flood her mind and heart. She'd forgotten how nice his dark brown hair complemented those Thornton blue eyes or how his manly features could melt the strongest of female hearts.

He did favor his brother, but in many ways, he was nothing like Nicholas.

Unfortunately, she had hoped he would be.

How could she forget he'd always been so nice and kind to her? His ready smile could lift her spirits, and his low, smooth voice would make her feel warm and welcome.

I can't do this, she thought in a panic. *He doesn't deserve what I'm going to do to him!*

Alarmed, she grabbed Theodora's arm. "This will not work!" she whispered harshly in her cousin's ear. "We have to leave. Now!"

"No!" Theodora answered, while she continued to walk toward their hosts. "It is all planned. There is no backing away from it!"

"Lady Montbatten! We are delighted you could come." Lady Beckingham greeted her warmly, forcing Katherine to walk forward into the room.

She swallowed hard and pasted on a smile. Nodding to her hosts, she answered, "Lord and Lady Beckingham, may I introduce you to my cousin, Miss Theodora Vine."

Introductions and greetings were made, and finally she and

Theodora were once again alone. "Theodora, please. I remember Thomas now that I have seen him. He is too nice—too good of a man to have this done to him!" Katherine pleaded.

Theodora turned and gave her a stern look—a look she did well since she stood so tall and had a long, hawkish nose from which to gaze down. "Think, Katherine! Think of how humiliated you have felt all these months. Think of how Nicholas Thornton has been happy in his grand estate with his new wife, while you've been alone with no prospects. Just think, dear, of how the men in the room stared at you when you walked in tonight." She smiled cunningly. "Why, they were almost sneering at you, Kate. You, who were once declared the 'original' of the entire *ton!* You cannot let this humiliation go unpunished. Can you?"

The hurt and bitter feelings flooded her mind. Indeed, she had noticed how they gawked at her tonight, but she tried not to dwell on it. As she glanced around the room, however, she could not let go of the truth of her circumstance.

She was ruined, and never would her reputation be spotless again.

It was all thanks to Nicholas Thornton. And if Theodora was correct, his brother was not completely innocent, either.

Somebody had to pay. Vengeance had to be taken on some level.

She looked to the back of the room, and her gaze lit on the handsome man standing beside the Duke of Northingshire.

"See how he does not seem to have a care in the world?" Theodora whispered softly in her ear. "He does not have to worry about what people are saying when he enters a room. He does not lie awake at night crying over his fate and how unfair his life has become."

"You're right," she said resolutely, studying his impeccable black suit with his snow white cravat tied neatly at his throat.

He and his brother were surely cut from the same cloth! Of course, Thomas would have known about Nicholas breaking their engagement. He did nothing to stop his brother and perhaps even had a hand in the decision. "Tonight our plan shall begin," she murmured more to herself.

Suddenly, he turned and caught her staring at him. Her doubts resurfaced, and she nearly turned around and ran out of the room. But the hurt and anger stirring in her heart made her stay where she was.

She refused to wonder why her heart seemed to pound so as his beautiful eyes met her own. She did not dare contemplate how handsome he was and how stately he appeared standing there against the dark blue wall of the room. She would not dare let herself believe she was attracted to the very man she had vowed to ruin by securing his affections, making him think she wanted to be his wife, then leaving him at the altar.

Tonight she would begin to avenge her honor.

Tonight Thomas Thornton would regret the day he ever met her.

With a slow curve of her lips, she smiled at him and began to walk his direction.

The plan was in motion. There was no backing out now.

two

Katherine had almost reached Thomas when suddenly Lord Malcolm Paisley, a tall, meticulously dressed man whose snobbery and condescension were only surpassed by his waspish tongue, blocked her path. A calculating smile curved his thin lips as he made a sweep of her figure while tugging on the delicate lace of his sleeve.

His eyes made her skin crawl.

"Dear Lady Katherine," he purred with sarcasm. "You appear quite a bit older since last we met. I should not have known you had I not heard your name announced."

Katherine felt the barb as she was meant to, since she'd seen him only two months ago, but was far too sophisticated to let Paisley know he'd hurt her. "Hmm." She gave him equal measure, letting her eyes scan his flashy attire. "I don't believe I shall take the opinion of a man who mixes pink with yellow."

He smiled, but Katherine could tell her words had irritated him. "Perhaps you should dull your tongue, my lady; otherwise, not even a poor farmer will want you for a wife." He made a snorting laugh that was not at all attractive. "Of course, after they hear of your scandalous past, they'll be likely to turn and run anyway."

"Tsk, tsk, Paisley." A deep voice sounded behind Katherine, and she knew right away it was Thomas Thornton. "I believe you've forgotten the correct manner in which to speak to a lady."

The sneer fell from Paisley's face as if someone had taken a big swipe and wiped it away. In its place was a simpering smile, typical behavior for him when he was confronted by a "favorite" of the *ton*. Paisley knew exactly whom he could sharpen his claws on and who would destroy him socially—and, in all probability, physically.

Thomas Thornton, former navy lieutenant and brother of the Earl of Kenswick, was one such man.

"Thornton! Can't tell you how glad we all were to know you were alive and well. Why, I was telling Crowler the other day—"

"I believe you owe Lady Katherine an apology, Paisley," he bluntly interrupted, causing the smaller man's neck to burn fiery red with anger.

Paisley tugged at his cuffs again. "I see you don't quite know the way of things, Thornton; but that is understandable since you have been away for quite some time."

"I understand if an apology is not offered in the next minute, then I shall be forced to—"

"Don't you dare say it!" Katherine hissed, cutting off what she knew was a threat of a duel between the two men. She glanced around and was somewhat relieved they had not drawn too much attention. "My reputation, as tattered as it is, cannot survive another scene between gentlemen. I beg you, please, Lord Thornton—let this go!" she implored Thomas.

A moment of strained silence passed as the two men contemplated one another; then Paisley backed down, grudgingly nodding to them both before turning away. They watched Paisley slink back to his circle of friends. As for Katherine, she was trying not to be moved by the way Thomas defended her.

"I thank you, my lord, for desisting in your argument with him. I have to be careful since—" She faltered as the bitterness rose up and threatened to make her cry. How could she go through with this charade when he was a constant reminder of what she'd lost?

"Since my brother broke your engagement," he finished for her with a weary sigh. "Would you like to take a turn about the terrace? I believe the fresh air would do us both good."

Katherine nodded, grateful for the chance to compose herself. But when they began to walk together toward the terrace doors, she realized they had become the object of everyone's attention.

He must have sensed her panic, for he put a steadying hand under her arm and guided her to their destination. "Relax," he whispered. "They shall soon lose interest."

He guided her to a stone bench, and when she had sat down, he stood beside her, leaning against the smooth railing. "Shall I get you something to drink?"

"No," she answered quickly. "I am fine, thank you."

He raised a brow as if he didn't believe her but refrained from saying so. "How long has this been going on?" he asked bluntly, forgoing any of the meaningless talk she'd expected.

She didn't pretend to misunderstand. "For quite a few months now, just before your brother remarried," she said, wincing that her words had sounded so bitter. Would the hurt of the situation ever go away?

"I wish I could help, Katherine. You know I have always held you in the highest esteem."

She turned her face away from him with a brittle smile. "That is what Nicholas wrote in a letter to me, right before he married that little vicar's daughter!" She stood and paced around the bench. "Of course, he also said he was sorry and wanted to make restitution. Well, if he truly wanted to do that, he could have reinstated the engagement and married me instead of that commoner!" she cried softly with her arms held out to her sides.

But as soon as those words left her mouth and she saw the dismay on Thomas's face, she regretted her outburst. What was she doing? She was supposed to be cozying up to him and drawing him into her life—getting him to like her.

Dropping back down to the bench, she covered her face with her hands, wishing she could leave. She knew, deep in her soul, she was not cut out for this revenge business. "I'm sorry. I should not have said—"

"Shh," Thomas whispered as he sat beside her, taking one of her gloved hands. "I know it has been a trying time, and I am truly sorry for it." She looked up at him, breathing in the light fragrance of his cologne and feeling the warmth of his closeness. Thomas was different from Nicholas in the way most second sons usually were. He did not have the seriousness or regal bearing the earl did; instead, he seemed more friendly, a man who didn't dwell too heavily on the problems around him. He was kind and had a ready smile, even after all he'd been through.

And this revelation again made her want to abandon the crazy plan to ruin him.

Suddenly Theodora was there, as if she'd sensed Katherine wavering. It was uncanny, really.

"Ah! There you are," Theodora spoke up in her nasal tone, though she was staring at Thomas and none too friendly.

Seeing Thomas's reaction to her was something like watching a cat's back bow up when a stranger approaches—only he never moved a muscle, except for the tightening of his jaw. He didn't like either her cousin or her interruption.

Thomas came instantly to his feet. "I don't believe we've been introduced," he announced imperially while peering down his nose at Theodora.

Katherine almost smiled when she realized Thomas *could* act like his brother when he wanted to.

She was musing over his extremely good looks when Theodora snapped her back to reality. "I am Theodora Vine, my lord."

Katherine's cheeks grew hot as she realized she'd been staring at Thomas and totally ignored his question. "Uh—yes! This is my cousin, my lord. She has been staying with us in town and will be going back with us to Ravenhurst Castle."

Thomas gave her a knowing expression and a grin. *The scoundrel!* He'd known she was admiring him! He looked back to Theodora, and all manner of pleasantness was gone from his face as he gave a short and snappy bow. "Miss Vine."

"I believe you, too, will be retiring to your country home, is that not right, my lord?" Theodora asked, and Katherine could tell he did not appreciate the prying question from one he knew so little. But after a pause, he answered, though not to Theodora.

He gazed directly into Katherine's eyes. "Indeed, I shall be there late tomorrow. I find it a most fortunate circumstance that you shall also be returning to your home, since they are but a stone's throw from each other." He glanced at her cousin as if annoyed she was there and listening so intently but then brought his attention back to Katherine.

Thomas paused a moment as if he wanted to say more, then decided against it. Instead, he picked up Katherine's hand and kissed the satin-covered knuckles. "It has been a pleasure, my lady."

To her cousin, he barely nodded his head. "Miss Vine," he murmured, then walked away.

Theodora waited until Thomas had entered the ballroom before she began her tirade. "What do you think you were doing out here alone with that man?"

Katherine was confused. "Dora, is not that the whole point of the evening—becoming reacquainted with him so he will begin courting me?"

Theodora's lips tightened, and her nose flared with displeasure. "Reacquainted, yes—but it seemed as though you two were almost in an embrace when I walked out here! Is your reputation not black enough?"

"What do you care of my reputation? It will be in tatters anyway after our plan is finished."

"But you will have the satisfaction of knowing vengeance has been served upon the Thornton family! Remember why we are doing this!" Theodora took a deep breath as if calming herself. "You want to appear interested in Lord Thornton so he will want to call on you once he has settled into Ravenhurst. He all but implied that was his intention, anyway! If you persist in coming on too strong, he will believe the rumors that have been spread about you!"

Theodora's words cut her deeply, as her cousin knew they would. She didn't deserve what had been done to her. She didn't deserve to have her hopes and dreams dashed.

But does Thomas deserve to have his own life trampled upon, either? a voice whispered in her head.

"Perhaps he already does believe them," Theodora said softly. Katherine looked up, her gaze going to the window through which her cousin was staring.

There she saw Thomas standing with Miss Claudia Baumgartner, an American girl who had just come to England to live with her grandfather, the Marquis of Moreland. At first she had been considered an oddity—a rustic. But, according to local gossip, she had charmed her critics and won over more than one heart of the elite *ton*.

Lord Thomas Thornton appeared completely captivated by her.

Katherine swallowed and refused to examine the strange feeling coursing through her as she watched Thomas smile at the girl.

It felt a lot like. . .jealousy.

"Don't just stand there, Kate!" Theodora charged, giving

her a stern look. "Go in there! Charm the man!"

Exasperated, Katherine shook her head. "First I'm coming on too strong, and now you are throwing me at him! He will think I am a lunatic if I seek him out now. It has been only a couple of minutes since we met."

Theodora shrugged her bony shoulders and tilted up her chin. "Do you want to have your revenge or not?"

Katherine sighed. "Of course, I do."

"You're correct, though, in saying you cannot just walk up to him." Theodora tapped a long, thin finger on her pointy chin, then smiled.

Katherine was disturbed at the coldness radiating from that smile.

"Give me your gloves!" she demanded, holding out her hands expectantly.

"What?"

Theodora all but growled, "Give me your gloves! I have a plan!"

Katherine reluctantly did as she bade. "I don't understand why—"

"Because you are going to walk past Thornton and 'accidentally' drop your glove. He'll pick it up, drawing attention away from the little American and onto you," she explained while straightening Katherine's gloves, then handing them back to her.

"That's the oldest trick in the book, Dora! He'll know right away it was no accident!"

"It's the oldest trick because it works, Kate," she explained as if she were talking to a child. "And it doesn't matter if he knows the truth or not. He will still be flattered you attempted such a ploy to grab his attention."

Katherine felt as though every eye in the room were watching her walk toward Thomas and waiting for her to make a fool of herself. She was mortified she was reduced to performing such tactics to draw a man's attention. Two years ago she had only to walk into a room and the gentlemen would be instantly at her side, competing for even a moment of her time.

How she longed for that life again.

Miss Baumgartner was staring up into Thomas's face, laughing at something he had just said, when she reached them. She had been hoping the glove trick would not be needed, that he would acknowledge her presence and be drawn to her side.

It was clearly not going to happen.

So, with a fortified breath and a glance about the room to make sure no one was looking, Katherine opened her hand, letting one of her long satin gloves drift to the ground at Thomas's feet.

She took one step, then two, and by the time she took the third, it dawned on her that he was not coming after her or calling out that she'd dropped her glove.

Nonchalantly, she stopped, and pretending to study the arrangement of flowers beside her, she carefully took a peek at where Thomas was standing.

There he was—still standing by Miss Baumgartner—still talking and smiling at the woman—completely ignorant of the fact her glove was lying at his feet.

Then it was under his feet as he moved a bit to take a glass of punch from a servant passing by.

Katherine wanted to cry. She peered past Thomas and saw Theodora glaring at her, then she truly wanted to cry.

With a resolve to go home no matter what her cousin said about it, Katherine turned quickly and took only one step before she crashed into the flower arrangement and the ceramic pedestal it sat upon.

The sound it made crashing into the marble floor was akin

to the blast of a cannon. Now she had not only Thomas's attention, but everyone else's as well.

"Are you all right?" Thomas asked as he put a steadying hand upon her back, his voice filled with concern.

Katherine glanced at him, then uneasily scanned the room at the curious and scandalized faces staring at her in fascination. *Is this what happens to those whose reputation is destroyed? Does their dignity leave them as well?* she thought wildly.

"I believe I feel faint," she lied and for the first time in her life fell into a pretend swoon.

Thomas, just as she knew he would, caught her perfectly, swept her into his arms and out of the Beckinghams' ballroom.

*

"You can open your eyes now. We are quite alone," Thomas whispered into Katherine's ear, as he stood in an empty corridor of Beckingham Hall, still holding the beautiful lady in his arms.

Her eyes came instantly open and gazed at him with unbelief. "You knew?"

Thomas grinned as he reluctantly lowered her to the ground. "I deduced you considered it the best possible action to take. And it worked. It got you out of the room and away from the curious stares of the *ton*," he said with a shrug.

Katherine laughed. "Am I that transparent?"

Thomas grinned. "Not a bit. I would never have imagined you would have dropped a glove at my feet, or I would have noticed it when it happened!"

He saw Katherine's face turn red, and she opened her mouth as if to speak, but nothing came out. He continued, "I found it after your dance with the flower arrangement."

Katherine covered her face with her hands. "That was possibly the stupidest thing I have ever done!"

Thomas stood staring at her for a moment, trying to sort

out the feelings that were swirling around in his mind where this enchanting woman was concerned. Never could he remember being so captivated.

He put his hand in his pocket and closed it around the smooth silk of the glove he'd scooped off the floor after her fall. He started to give it back to her, but for some reason unknown to him, he let it go.

"I would never call you stupid, my lady. Clever, smart, beautiful, and even enchanting maybe," he teased as he pulled her hands away from her face.

Katherine glanced up at him, then quickly turned away with embarrassment. "I suppose you are wondering why I would do such a thing."

"No," Thomas stated firmly, causing her to bring her gaze back to his. "I prefer to find that answer when we return to Derbyshire."

A myriad of emotions passed over her face, most of which Thomas could not decipher.

"What—are you saying, my lord?" she asked carefully.

"I am asking if I might call on you the day after tomorrow. Shall we say ten in the morning?"

The dread he saw in her eyes when that question left his lips had him truly baffled. But it disappeared as quickly as it had arisen. "Indeed, my lord. My family and I shall eagerly anticipate it," she told him formally. "Now if you'll excuse me, I must go find my cousin so we may leave."

"Yes, of course," he murmured as he watched her hasten away.

Thomas stood there for a moment, puzzled as to her quick change of mood. One moment she appeared to show genuine interest in him; the next, she became cold and proper!

It was a mystery he was determined to solve! He'd have ample time at Rosehaven to get to know Katherine a little better and find out if possibly she was the right woman for him.

He then thought of his son, Ty, and wondered how she would respond to the toddler. That was also an important consideration in his quest for a wife.

A quest he now hoped and prayed would end with Lady Katherine Montbatten as his wife.

three

"I think perhaps I should tell you something I'm not sure you are going to like," Katherine began as she stood before her parents in their elegantly furnished drawing room two days after the ball. The gentle candlelight shining through the crystal lamps about the room should have been soothing to her nerves, but until she finished this meeting, nothing would help. She had wanted to avoid telling them of Thomas's visit, but knowing he would probably want to speak to them, she had to prepare them.

"Do sit down, dear, while you tell us. It is giving my poor neck an ache having to look up at you," her mother, Lady Montbatten, complained as she waved about a lace handkerchief she was rarely without.

Stifling a sigh because of her mother's frequent complaining, Katherine sat down on the blue velvet settee across from her parents. Still dreading to tell her parents the news, she took a moment to smooth the cream taffeta of her day dress.

"Well, spit it out, girl!" her father's loud voice boomed, causing her, her mother, and her sister, who was pretending to read a book, to jerk. His tall, large stature frightened those who didn't know him, but all his friends and family knew that underneath his austere gruffness, he was quite a marshmallow.

"Yes, well, I need to tell you someone will be coming to call here this morning," Katherine started again, unable to blurt out the news as she wanted.

"Who, dear?" her mother asked when Katherine did not finish.

"A man, Mama. A man who will come to call on—me."

A loud, thoroughly irate sigh came from the duke as he slapped his large hand on the delicate wooden arms of the chair, making her mother frown with disapproval. "Is this to be a game of 'charades' or 'question and answer'? Say what you must and cease shilly-shallying!"

"Lord-Thomas-Thornton-is-the-man!" she all but yelled in one quick breath. "There! It is said!"

"Dear, a proper lady does not raise her voice so—"

"Margaret, please! Did you not hear what she just told us?" her father interrupted, his voice sounding stunned.

Her mother's eyes widened. "Lord Thomas Thornton, did you say?" She fell back in her chair, waving her hand in front of her face in a frantic motion. "I do believe I might need my smelling salts. Lucinda, please ring for Amelia to bring them," she ordered Katherine's little sister.

Lucinda, or "Lucy" as most everyone called her, showed her displeasure at having to leave the room by loudly plopping her book down on an end table and making a huffing noise. "I do not understand why I am always sent on one errand or another to do everyone's bidding!" She whirled dramatically after opening the door, then paused. "Isn't that what we have servants for?" she cried and, without waiting for an answer, flounced out of the room in typical twelve-year-old fashion.

"That girl must be taken in hand! She has grown so very wild in the last year." Her mother groaned, still in her semireclined condition. "We must see to finding her a new governess."

"Yes, yes, all that can be dealt with later, but let's get back to the subject at hand," Lord Montbatten complained impatiently, still staring at his daughter. "How is it you've become acquainted with the Thorntons again, Daughter? I would have thought you would have found any connection with that family distasteful and even hurtful."

If her father only knew the truth of how she had deliberately sought out Thomas Thornton, of how she planned to ruin his family's name. "We met at the Beckingham ball, Papa, two nights ago. We were always friends, you know, before"— she faltered, then continued—"before the incident."

The duke continued to frown, and Katherine became distinctly uncomfortable under his penetrating gaze. "Are you saying you would welcome his suit if he should choose to pursue you?"

No! she wanted to cry. She wanted nothing to do with anyone from the Thornton family. But she could not say that. Minutes before she'd met with her parents, Theodora had reminded her—strongly—of her purpose, her mission.

"What would you say, Papa, if I said yes?" she asked instead.

Katherine had expected her father to vehemently oppose any sort of match between Thomas and her. In fact, part of her secretly wished he would, so she wouldn't have to go through with the plan.

"Why, I think it is a marvelous turn of events!" Lord Montbatten crowed, lifting his arms in a triumphal gesture. "I had despaired of your ever receiving another offer for your hand, and the fact it is Lord Thornton's brother makes the whole affair work to our advantage!"

Katherine frowned. "Papa, he is just coming to call, not pledging his troth, and how would his pursuing me work to our advantage?"

"It will speak loudly to all the *ton* if the Earl of Kenswick's brother shows his favor to you; then all those rumors about you and the duel will be unfounded. Don't you see—if they were true and Kenswick did throw you over because of something you did, then his brother wouldn't speak to you, much less come to call!"

Katherine sat there stunned as her father's words sank into

her. To think her reputation could be restored simply by being seen with Lord Thomas Thornton. The need to ruin him and his family would no longer be necessary. All she would have to do was be seen with Thomas, making it clear she was not interested in marriage, and in a month or two, they could go their separate ways.

Her reputation would be restored, and there would no longer be a need for the plan.

"You are right, Papa, even though I had not thought of it that way," she murmured as the excitement of her new idea took root.

"But you must, darling!" her mother chimed in, apparently fully recovered from her swoon without the aid of smelling salts. "Since the breakup of your engagement, it has been hard on all of us, especially me." She fell back in her chair again, laying her hand over her forehead. "Being snubbed at every gathering can be quite vexing on my fragile health!"

Shaking her head and stopping short of rolling her eyes, Katherine retorted, "It is my aim in life, Mama, to put right every wrong in my life so that it might benefit your own."

The sarcasm breezed right over her mother's flighty head. "I appreciate that, dear. Truly I do."

Katherine and her father shared a wry glance, then stood. "If you both will excuse me, I had better freshen up before Lord Thornton arrives."

"Yes, do make yourself extra presentable, dear. We can't lose this one, you know. It might be quite some time before another comes to call!" her mother said, her voice shaky with false bravado. "If you happen to pass Lucinda in the hall, can you please tell her to rush with those salts, dear?"

"Yes, Mama," she said in a singsong voice as she hurried from the room.

It was Theodora's room she ran to, however, instead of her

own. "Dora! I have just met with my parents, and Papa made the most excellent point!" Excitedly, she told her cousin what her father had said. "So you see, Dora, we do not have to carry out this plan to the bitter end! Just being seen with Lord Thornton will boost my reputation."

"No!" Theodora practically screamed at her as she stood and took Katherine by the arm. "You must see this plan through— you must! It's the only way we—I mean, you—can be fully vindicated!"

Katherine became alarmed at Theodora's anxiety. She had not expected such a response. "But we do not have to ruin Thomas to be vindicated. Just getting my good name back would be—"

"Enough? Is that what you were going to say?" Theodora spat. "Enough for all the turmoil you have been through? Enough for having your heart broken into a million pieces?"

Katherine knew the breakup of the engagement was more of a humiliation than a heartbreak, but her cousin seemed in no mood to hear that. She seemed quite—vexed!

"Dora, I just think this would be so much simpler—"

"We will stick with the plan, Kate. We must if we are to see all made right! We must!"

Katherine backed away from her, pulling her arm out of her painful grasp, and walked to the window. Confusion crowded her mind and heart as she wrestled with the dilemma.

Two riders on horses appeared in her line of vision, and she focused to reveal their identity. The two handsome men were dressed for riding in their fine suits, both expertly handling their mounts as they rode up the path.

It was Thomas and North, the Duke of Northingshire.

❧

"Are you absolutely sure you want to pursue this?" North asked Thomas again for the third time as they rode toward

Ravenhurst Castle. "Many other women would be glad to be your wife and the mother to your son."

"Yes, but there is something about Katherine I must follow up on. There was such a strong connection between us that I cannot help but think God had something to do with our meeting again."

And he was yearning to see her again.

four

"Three days, Dora! Three days have passed since I last saw Lord Thornton! Not that his visit to Ravenhurst was very memorable, since he stayed for only a few moments!" Katherine complained as she paced before Theodora. The cousins had been strolling in the park and had stopped to rest—at least one of them was resting. Katherine found she could not. "We have ridden or walked to this park not once but two times a day, and nothing!" She threw her arms up in exasperation. "I must have said something to put him off. Did I not make it clear I was interested in meeting him again?"

Theodora scanned the area around them and frowned with disapproval toward Katherine. "The whole village will know you are interested if you speak any louder."

Katherine stopped and returned the glare with one of her own. "Do not scold me as if I'm a child, Dora. My nerves have been so on edge this week that I fear turning into my mother!" She flounced herself down in a most unladylike manner, not caring one whit whether Dora disapproved or not. "And, speaking of my parents, have you not heard for yourself their conversations of a wedding between Thomas and me that will never take place? It's a terrible prospect to bear, Cousin, knowing I shall break their hearts when I refuse to marry him."

Dora reached over and gave her hand a brief pat. Katherine knew even this little show of affection was a stretch for her rather cool cousin. "We'll cross that bridge when we arrive at it, Kate. We need to focus our concern now on Lord Thornton and how we can get his attention."

Katherine stood again, too jittery to sit still. "Oh, why can we not forget about this stupid plan? I know I was all for it when we first spoke of it, but I did not realize how taxing it would be on all concerned."

Katherine was watching a lady enter the park pushing a baby carriage when she heard Theodora's sigh. "When it is over and you have been vindicated, you will thank me," she claimed, just as she always did when Katherine began to have doubts.

Katherine thought of something else. "But what of my parents? They are ecstatic I am being sought by Thomas! They will disown me when I deliberately do not show for my own wedding!"

"Then you must plant doubts about his character in their minds," Theodora reasoned.

"What about his character could I say? He has shown to be a gentleman in all things."

"He has not called on you in three days, Katherine. Start with that. Say he often neglects you and, if nothing else, lie."

Katherine got a sick feeling in her stomach. "I'm not very good at lying," she said quietly as she turned and looked back across the park.

"Then learn," was Theodora's harsh reply. "You can do this, Kate. You *must* do this."

"I don't know," she murmured, her attention becoming more drawn to the woman who had stopped the carriage and was taking the toddler into her arms.

"What don't you know?" Theodora demanded as she got up from her seat and came to stand by her.

"Dora, who is that lady?"

Theodora barely glanced over, clearly disinterested. "I have no idea, Katherine, but can we—"

"He's such a beautiful child, isn't he? And those dark brown curls are precious! I must go and have a closer look!" She started across the park, but her cousin grabbed her arm.

"What can you be thinking, Katherine? We don't even know who she is! What if she is from a family that is beneath our attention?"

Katherine pulled her arm away from Theodora's grasp and shot her a pointed expression. "I did not realize you had become such a snob, Dora. I will only be a minute. You do not have to accompany me."

"And I shan't!" her cousin called after her.

Katherine walked across the small park to where the lady was now watching the child play with a ball while sitting on the grass.

"Hello," Katherine greeted her. Now that she was closer, she saw the lady was dressed in conservative black like that of a nanny or governess. "I couldn't help but admire the child and had to come over for a closer look."

The woman peered up at Katherine, and her eyes grew big with recognition. She stood at once and bobbed a curtsy. "My lady! It is a stupendous honor to make your stupendous acquaintance. Just stupendous!"

Katherine was momentarily nonplussed, but she recovered. "Well—I see you know who I am. May I have the honor of knowing your name?"

She was presented with another of the woman's incredibly big smiles. "Indeed, my lady. I am Mrs. Sanborne, employed as a nanny for the young Master Tyler Thornton."

Katherine was glad the woman chose that moment to bend down and pick up the child because, for an instant, she could not speak—so shocked was she from that bit of news. "Would his father perchance be Lord Thomas Thornton, ma'am?" she asked breathlessly.

"Yes, he is, my lady." She hugged the smiling child to her, and for the first time, Katherine got a good look at the boy. Of course, he was Thomas's child. There was no mistaking his "Thornton" blue eyes.

"I know Lord Thornton, but this is the first time I've met his son," she told the lady, still gazing upon the sweet child. Every maternal feeling in her body reached out to the boy who was now motherless in this world with only his father and nanny to care for him.

You could be his mother, a voice whispered in her head, and for a moment, she let herself think about how it would be. How lovely it would be.

"May I hold him, do you think?" she asked impulsively.

Mrs. Sanborne was taken aback briefly. "Of course, my lady. But watch those pretty pearls you are wearing. He's broken a necklace or two of my own!"

"You wouldn't break my necklace, would you, dear boy? Oh, my, you are a handsome young man!" she crooned and was startled when Ty did reach out to grab her necklace. She caught him just in time. "Why, you are a little scamp!" She kissed his soft curls. "And you are so much like your father," she added.

"Are you saying I am a scamp also, my lady?" A deep, teasing voice sounded behind them, and she turned to find Thomas standing there, dressed handsomely in brown and light beige, his feet shod with his black shining Hessians.

With both the piercing eyes and his brilliant smile focused solely on Katherine, she found it very hard to answer without stumbling over her words. "I think you can be a scamp on occasion, my lord," she said slowly, thankful she was holding on to her composure.

Thomas threw his head back and laughed. "If you ask my brother, he will agree with you!"

His words were like a shower of cold water suddenly

thrown on them. Only young Ty seemed not to be disturbed by it as he laughed at his father, clapping his little chubby hands together.

Thomas reached out and fluffed his son's hair affectionately. "I did not mean—" he began.

"No, please," she interrupted. "I do not want you to feel as if you cannot mention him when we are together. I am quite over our breakup, I assure you," she lied, all the while wishing her words were the truth.

He smiled, but his eyes told her he wasn't quite convinced. "Well, I see you have become acquainted with my son," he said, changing the subject. "What do you think of him?"

Katherine smiled down at the little boy, who was once again trying to reach the pearls around her neck. "I think he's quite the little gentleman." She paused for effect while glancing up at Thomas. "Despite having a father who loves to tease defenseless women!"

Thomas put a finger to his lips. "Shh—he thinks I'm the perfect father. Wouldn't want to spoil the illusion, you know," he added with a wink.

Ty suddenly wanted his father and, giving a disgruntled cry, held out his chubby arms to Thomas. Katherine was startled when Thomas plucked the toddler out of her arms and swung him up in the air making "da-da" noises, causing his son to laugh with glee.

She had never seen a gentleman carry on like that with a baby. Not even her own father. Most left the rearing to the mother or nannies until the child was of age to learn, and then it meant hunting or schooling.

She was. . .enchanted.

⁂

Thomas found himself intrigued with the elusive Katherine. When he'd come up and seen her holding his son with that much affection, he'd hardly been able to bear it.

It had been his main worry—whether Katherine would accept his son. He'd even worried she might not care for children. But all those fears had dissipated the moment he'd walked up and found her holding Ty as if he were her own.

Thomas had missed her in the three days they had been apart, but he'd been so confused at her odd behavior. He wanted to pursue her but sensed a strong pull inside him urging him to be careful.

He'd been praying lately about the course he should take and where God was leading him. It was the reason he'd stayed home at Rosehaven. Until he knew what God wanted him to do, he did not want to chance meeting Katherine, letting his attraction to her override God's will.

The more he sought God's council, however, the more he felt God had brought Katherine into his life and he should try to discern her true feelings for him.

So, with the latter thought in mind, he'd finally ventured out and journeyed into town on the sincere hope of seeing Katherine there.

His hopes had soon become a reality.

There, under the cover of the large elms, she stood out like a glistening gem in her pale green dress and her hair swirled up in curls with some falling about her face. He knew the moment she looked up at him with her mysterious golden eyes that he'd fallen in love with her.

It stunned and humbled him all at once.

He hardly knew her. He'd known her only as his brother's fiancée, then the few moments he'd spent with her at the ball and at her parents' home.

But he so much wanted to know her better.

If only she weren't so. . .elusive! If only she were consistent with her actions and outward emotions, then he might not hesitate to ask for her hand, even at this early stage.

It wasn't uncommon, even for those couples who had met only once, to enter into an agreement of marriage. He'd done it himself with his first wife.

But he wanted this marriage to be different. He knew he loved Katherine and would do all he could to show his love to her, but he couldn't be sure of her feelings. He wouldn't enter another marriage where love was only one-sided, as his first marriage had been. It wouldn't be fair to either of them.

After Thomas had taken Ty from Katherine's arms and had him settled onto his side, he noticed she was smiling at him in wonder.

"What?" he asked curiously.

She shook her head. "I'm just amazed at your freedom of expression with your son, my lord."

"You don't like it?"

She smiled a smile that made his heart ache. "I think it's quite wonderful. I'd love to know the father of my children would treat our children the way you do yours," she explained, her voice wistful.

Thomas took a chance. "Perhaps you will have what you desire after all."

A strange moment passed between them when he spoke those words. A million emotions seemed to play across her expressive, dainty features. Thomas thought among them were happiness, wonderment, and—uneasiness? But that made no sense. What would cause her to feel uneasy with him?

"Perhaps," she finally answered, her eyes no longer focused on him but on his son, instead.

Thomas wanted to shake her as he realized she'd once again distanced herself from him.

"It has been good seeing you this morning, my lord, and meeting your son." She backed away. "I believe Dora must be wondering what has happened to me."

Thomas didn't want her to leave, not before he could figure out why she behaved the way she did. "Tea!" he blurted out, then winced when he realized how silly that sounded.

"I beg your pardon?"

"Have tea with me—at Rosehaven—this afternoon," he stammered. "You may bring your sister and your mother, also." Then as an afterthought, he added, "Oh, and your cousin may come along, too."

She paused, then shook her head with regret. "I fear I will have to decline your kind offer, my lord. My brother is coming home for a small holiday from Cambridge and will arrive at Ravenhurst today. I must be there to greet him."

"Ah, I understand. Perhaps another day," he told her, disappointed he would not see her later on.

Indecision played across her pretty features, and Thomas could tell she was trying to decide something. "My lord—" she began.

"Please, call me Thomas."

She sighed. "Thomas," she repeated. "I would extend to you an invitation to our small gathering tonight, but—"

Thomas held out his free hand, palm toward her. "Please, do not explain. Your family will want to be alone with your brother."

She shook her head and reached out and took hold of his hand, surprising him to his core. "It is not that, Thomas. I fear what Cameron might do if he sees you. He's been very upset about the whole scandal, you see. We've always been close, and he blames your brother and your family for what has befallen me."

Thomas lowered his hand, turning it slightly so he could hold onto hers. "Might I try to talk to him? Perhaps I could ease some of his anger."

"I don't know, Thomas. He grows furious every time your family's name is mentioned." It was then she realized she was holding his hand. Her eyes widened as she viewed their hands, and her cheeks were burning when she finally looked up at him.

Hastily, she pulled her hand away and backed up a few steps. "I–I think per–perhaps I'd better go," she stammered, clearly out of sorts from the encounter.

Thomas felt oddly elated by her reaction to him—first the spontaneity of holding his hand, and now the embarrassment of being caught.

"Of course. Give my regards to your family," he replied smoothly, holding back a grin.

She kept backing up until she bumped into a tree. She was quick to regain her composure as befit a duke's daughter. "Yes, uh—good-bye."

"My, she is quite a stupendous young lady, my lord," Mrs. Sanborne spoke as they both watched Katherine dash back to where her cousin was waiting for her. Thomas had completely forgotten about his son's nanny and wondered if she'd over-heard their conversation.

"Indeed, she is, Mrs. Sanborne. Indeed, she is."

"It is a pity you will not be able to take tea with her this stupendous afternoon. Perhaps you should call on her tomorrow. I would be stupendously surprised if she is not hoping for such a visit."

Thomas hid a smile as he continued to look in Katherine's direction. Mrs. Sanborne didn't seem to realize servants were not supposed to converse with their employers as if they were good friends. He rather liked it, though.

"I think I shall not visit tomorrow, Mrs. Sanborne, but wait until church on Sunday," Thomas replied. Perhaps seeing her family in a safe haven like the church would put the future

Duke of Ravenhurst in a better frame of mind for their first meeting.

"Oh, indeed, sir!" Mrs. Sanborne cried. "Absence does make the heart grow fonder, my mother often said."

This time Thomas laughed aloud, unable to hide his mirth at his governess's unusual way of looking at things. "Perhaps your dear mother was correct, Mrs. Sanborne. We shall see, won't we?"

He took one last glance at Katherine before leaving the park. At that moment, she, too, looked back at him. One second passed, then two. Thomas caught his breath for the brief span that she gazed at him, and his heart felt as though it were racing away.

It was soon over when she turned and followed her cousin deeper into the wooded area of the park. Thomas turned, also—his heart filled with hope she would soon be his bride.

five

"God must surely be vexed with me," Katherine whispered to Theodora as they sat in the small village abbey on Sunday morning.

Theodora's patience was clearly reaching the straining point as her thin nostrils flared. "It is only a sermon," she stressed.

Katherine shook her head, a panicked feeling building in her chest. "It is a sign, Dora! It must be!"

"Shh!" Lady Montbatten admonished, causing both ladies to face immediately toward the vicar.

As the vicar spoke on how Joseph forgave his brothers for their betrayal and how it paralleled the betrayal of Jesus, and yet He also forgave, Katherine leaned again toward Theodora.

"It is a sign from God!" she repeated in a whisper.

"Angels appearing out of nowhere are a sign. Dreams as Joseph had are a sign. Sermons are not!" She shook her head. "Now hush and peek around to see if Lord Thomas has arrived."

Though not convinced by Theodora's words, Katherine pretended to adjust her bonnet, giving her the chance to glance about. Upon meeting Thomas's gaze, Katherine turned back so quickly, she earned another disapproving look from her mother.

Thomas, as usual, appeared very handsome sitting beside North. She had noticed he wore a dark green coat and his hair was slightly disheveled, possibly done so by the breezy morning she'd also experienced when riding in their open carriage to the abbey.

"He's here," she told her cousin under her breath.

"Excellent," Theodora answered, still giving the impression of listening to the vicar, her lips curved in a satisfied grin.

Katherine, too, looked back at the vicar, but unlike her cousin, she could not sit there calmly and not feel the meaning of his sermons and the guilt it rained down on her soul. And now that she knew Thomas was only a few feet from her, the feelings were compounded. She tried to take calming breaths but found it did not help. Suddenly, she could take it no more. Jumping up from her seat, Katherine all but stumbled past her family to the aisle, then hurried out the door, not daring to acknowledge Thomas as she passed him.

Katherine ran until she reached a small grove of trees, then with a heartfelt groan fell to the fresh green grass. Covering her face with her hands, she wished she could cry and release all the pent-up feelings that had been building in her heart—the bitterness, anger, betrayal, and, lately, guilt.

But she couldn't, and she thought maybe she didn't deserve the luxury of a good cry—not when she was set on a course that was so contrary to her character.

"Are you all right?" a voice asked from up above her. A voice she knew was Thomas's.

And for some reason, Katherine became highly irritated at his presence. Lowering her hands, she peered up to find his handsome face swathed with worry and concern. "Are you always like this?" she blurted out, her tone none too friendly.

He froze for a moment, seemingly stunned by her abruptness. "I beg your pardon?"

She stood up, ignoring his outstretched hand. "Do you always do the right things?" When he continued to appear puzzled, she let out a breath of frustration. "Are you always such a gentleman? Do you ever do anything—well—*wrong*?"

He studied her, then asked carefully, "Katherine, are you

feeling all right? Perhaps I could see you home so you might lie down for a—"

"I am not sick!" she interrupted, childishly stomping one foot. "What I am trying to ask is if you are always this nice? Do you ever say the wrong thing or do something you are not proud of—"

"Are you saying you want me to act ungentlemanly?" he interrupted this time.

Katherine rolled her eyes as she threw her arms up in frustration. "Are you mad? Why would I want that?"

Thomas opened and closed his mouth twice before any words came out. "I don't think *I* am the mad one!" he finally answered, his deep voice calm though highly strained.

Katherine knew she was sounding like a lunatic, but like a cart rolling down a hill, she could not seem to stop! "Ha! There, you see! You have insulted me!" She folded her arms and smiled smugly, glad finally to find some nibble of ammunition she could use against him. "You do not always do or say the right thing after all!"

Thomas surprised her by letting out a wry chuckle. "My lady, are you always this conflicting? First you are dropping gloves at my feet and crashing into vases; next you are cuddling my son as if he were your own." He paused. "A sight, I might add, that took my breath away and gave me great hopes for the future." He smiled and reached for her gloved hand. "Then finally you are berating me for being a gentleman and smile when you think I am not one. All this makes no sense to me, but I must say I find it quite enjoyable!"

Katherine took a swift breath as he bent his head over her hand, kissing her knuckles gently, sending a wave of excitement to her heart.

Then a loud voice, which could only belong to her bratty sister, broke their moment. "I see Mama's fears are to be realized!"

Lucy declared as she stood there with her arms folded and her eyes narrowed suspiciously upon their clasped hands.

Katherine quickly stepped back, snatching her hand away and holding it behind her as if she were hiding it. "Lucy! Why aren't you in church?" she demanded, chagrined to find her voice slightly breathy. She could only hope she wasn't visibly blushing!

"Why aren't you?" her sister shot back.

"I had to, well, I"—she stumbled for an excuse—"I had to get a bit of fresh air!" She lifted her chin and gave her sister equal measure on her stare.

She should have known better than to get into a verbal challenge with her sister. Lucy, though only twelve, could outsmart and outtalk most of the Montbatten family when she chose to.

"And I suppose you needed Lord Thornton to help you find the fresh air?" she questioned smoothly while shifting her sharp gaze to Thomas.

Katherine now knew she was blushing. Her cheeks were practically on fire! "Lucy! Can you please go back to the abbey—"

"If I go, you must go with me," she interrupted. "Mama and Papa sent me to be your chaperone."

Katherine groaned and looked over at Thomas, who grinned. "There is a very fine incline over there that is shaded and grassy. Why don't we wait over there until your parents can join us?" Thomas suggested.

Katherine was surprised when he extended his arm not only to her but to Lucy as well. For the first time, Katherine saw Lucy blush as she took his arm, gazing up at him with adoring eyes. Even Lucy, apparently, was not immune to Thomas's charm.

Fine, Katherine thought. Not only would she have to deal

with her parents after the whole ordeal was over with, but she'd also have to contend with her sister's feelings.

Once they were seated, Lucy stated, "You do know our parents are all quite giddy about your interest in my sister."

"Indeed!" Thomas sputtered with a shocked laugh.

Katherine was behind him, dismayed as well, but she was not laughing! "Lucinda Ann Montbatten! Ladies do not say such—"

"We'd all thought her as 'on the shelf,' an old maid, forever without a hus—"

"I think he understands your meaning, Lucy. Now, please—" Katherine tried to silence her again, even attempting to reach across Thomas to give her a pinch of warning, but it did no good. Thomas merely plucked her hand and folded it into his own and encouraged Lucy to continue.

Ignoring Katherine's outraged gasp, Lucy did as he asked. "As I was saying, we thought her doomed to a life alone until, of course, you came along, my lord." She gave him another smile, and Katherine thought she might have even winked at him, but she could not be sure.

"Ah! Just like a fairytale, wouldn't you say, Katherine?" Thomas teased, smiling into her perturbed stare, holding fast to her hand when she tried to pull away.

"Yes, that is exactly what Mama said. She also said she hoped you wouldn't wait long to propose, since you were Kate's only chance for matrimony and she did not want anything to happen to run you off."

This time Katherine managed to pull free of Thomas's hold. Leaping to her feet, she shook her finger at Lucy, who was now trying to scoot behind Thomas for protection. "You will end up in the same situation, Sister dear, if you don't act in a more ladylike manner!" Katherine shrieked.

By now Katherine was so angry, she forgot to mind her own

behavior. All she could think of was getting her hands on her big-mouthed sibling. Twice she circled around the man as her sister kept scrambling away from her.

Then, in a moment of triumph, Katherine caught her. "Ha! I've got you. Now what are you going to do?" she growled as she tugged her sister by the arm and glared down into her panicked face.

But then the panic turned to glee as Lucy focused on something beyond Katherine. "Mama! Papa! Help me!" she yelled in a pitiful voice. "Katherine was angry because I caught the two of them in a kiss, and now she is trying to harm me!"

Katherine knew she'd been bested. But it wasn't the fact that her parents were there to witness her unladylike behavior—they'd seen her and Lucy get into tussles before. No, it was because she suddenly noticed Thomas watching her, doing all he could to hold back his laughter!

"Katherine! I say, Daughter, your behavior is not at all befitting your station!" her father scolded in his booming voice as he kept glancing with apprehension to Thomas.

"Uh, yes, dear! We don't want to give anyone the wrong impression, do we?" her mother seconded, emphasizing each word in her last sentence while motioning toward Thomas with a nonsubtle movement of her head.

Thomas chose to rise at that moment, giving her parents a brief bow. "Your graces," he greeted them with a dashing smile. "Trust me when I say there is nothing Katherine could do to change my good opinion of her." Thomas turned his gaze to her, and she felt the power of his tender smile all the way to her toes. "I think she is the most beautiful, most fascinating woman I have ever met."

Katherine was barely aware of her parents crowing with approval and flattery aimed at Thomas, for she was momentarily struck blind and deaf from all else in the world except Lord

Thomas Thornton—a man Katherine was beginning to realize was a most extraordinary man, indeed. A fact she wished with all her heart she'd known before making her ill-fated plans.

What would it be like, she wondered, if he were to be her fiancé in truth? What would it be like to make plans for the future with this man in it?

"Did anyone hear me when I said I caught them kissing?" Lucy called out, breaking the connection that had been flowing between them.

Katherine opened her mouth to defend herself when Thomas spoke. "I beg your pardon, your graces, but I was only kissing Katherine's hand." He smiled a charming smile at her mother. "Her *gloved* hand, at that."

Katherine watched her mother gush with glee. "Of course, we suspected nothing else," Lady Montbatten assured him, waving her lacy handkerchief in his direction. "But I was young once, my lord, and I do know what it's like when you are"—she paused for effect—"in love?"

Katherine watched in wonder as Thomas handled her prying with cunning. "Your grace, one would only have to gaze upon your fair skin to suppose those memories were not so long ago," he told her smoothly.

Lady Montbatten giggled into her handkerchief like a schoolgirl, and Katherine realized she was actually feeling jealous of her mother!

It was at that moment Theodora arrived, followed by North.

"Cousin." Theodora spoke first. "We've been all over the church grounds trying to locate you," she told Katherine. "Is everything all right?"

Katherine resented Theodora's prying question and curious expression. In fact, Katherine was beginning to wonder how she could convince Theodora they should not go through with their plan.

But even if she did achieve that difficult task, how would she ever convince her cousin she might just *want* Thomas to ask her to marry him? She might just want everything about their relationship to be—real.

Katherine sighed. That line of thought would require more reflection, however. Now she would just pretend to go along with Theodora.

"Of course, everything is all right," Katherine answered. "We were just about to come and find you."

"Actually," Thomas inserted, causing all eyes to turn toward him, "I thought perhaps you'd like to join me for a picnic in my garden. It is so beautiful this time of year, and the roses are beginning to bloom." He nodded toward her parents to make sure they knew they were to be included.

"What a delightful suggestion, my lord!" Lady Montbatten crooned, clapping her hands together. "We would be honored, wouldn't we, Raven?" she spoke to her husband using his nickname from his title of Duke of Ravenhurst.

"Capital idea!" the duke seconded with a satisfied smile. "I'll send a servant to inform Cameron of our plans, and we will meet you at the noon hour."

Thomas nodded. "Cameron is, of course, invited, also."

The Montbattens all exchanged uneasy glances. "I think we shall wait until another day to include our son," Lord Montbatten finally answered.

"If you think it best."

The duke frowned. "Trust me—it is best."

"On second thought, my dear, why don't we send Theodora to give Rogers the message?" Lady Montbatten chimed in, referring to their footman waiting for them at the abbey. "Rosehaven is not too far, and it will give us a chance to talk more, don't you agree?"

Katherine saw her mother send her father a significant look, and he was a little slow at catching its meaning but soon did. "Well, I had not wanted to walk—uh—but, of course—I think the walk would be a wonderful idea," he answered slowly and carefully. "Run along, Theodora, and see to Rogers, will you?"

Katherine knew Theodora did not like being treated like the poor relative she was. Though she was treated better and more equal than most, she was still Katherine's companion, totally dependent on the generosity of the duke and duchess.

With her pinched lips and pointy chin thrust high in the air, Theodora stalked away, but her displeasure had not gone unnoticed. Katherine saw her father frowning after her, so she turned his attention elsewhere.

"What about your son?" she asked Thomas brightly.

It was North who answered. "I sent them along in the carriage. They should be waiting for us at Rosehaven."

Thomas nodded, motioning ahead on the path. "Then let's meet them, shall we?"

As they began to walk, Katherine found herself walking in front with Thomas, Lucy was paired with North, and her mother and father brought up the rear. The silence between them all was quite comfortable as they strolled along the tree-lined path with the sweet smell of the spring flowers drifting upon the light breeze.

Lucy apparently didn't think so, though. As usual, she spoke exactly what was on her mind. "It is really quite odd to be walking with you, my lord, when just last year we were attending your funeral," she commented, referring to the time when his ship had gone down during the war and he'd been declared dead.

Both Katherine and her parents scolded the girl at one time. "Lucinda! Do not say another word!" "Please be quiet!" "Hush—"

"It is quite all right," Thomas interrupted, turning slightly to smile at the precocious girl. "Of course, it must seem odd to her."

Katherine turned to see her mother dabbing frantically at her forehead with her handkerchief. "Yes, but she should not say so aloud. It is quite unbecoming! Quite!" her mother emphasized, her voice shaking with embarrassment.

"Why shouldn't I say so aloud? He is alive, isn't he? I should think he would be glad to talk about it," Lucy insisted. "What do you think about it, North?" she directed her question to her walking companion.

"Your grace, Lucy. You must address him as 'your grace'!" Lady Montbatten admonished.

Lucy let out a sound of disgust and rolled her eyes. "What do you think about it—*your grace!*"

North chuckled. "I think we are blessed to have Thomas among us. Our sorrow was turned to great gladness when he came home to us."

"I know my parents are glad about it. At least they are now since he's been courting my sister!"

More instantaneous scolding came from Katherine and her parents. But Thomas's laugh interrupted them all with surprise. "Was there much crying at the memorial service, Lucy? Were pretty words spoken on my behalf?" he asked in a teasing voice.

Lucy nodded seriously. "Oh, yes. And I'm sure I would have cried over you, too, had I known you better then."

Thomas's laughter again stopped Lucy from being scolded too much, but Katherine knew she must have a talk with her sister as soon as possible on proper conversation etiquette.

Katherine felt compelled to put an end to their talk of death and funerals. "I am sure you will not have to worry about crying over Thomas for a great many years. I am sure God will see fit to give him a long life after all he has been through."

She peered up at Thomas to give him a quick smile, but when she found him looking back at her with such a tender expression, she nearly stumbled with its impact.

"Indeed, I pray you are correct. I have a whole life I want to experience before I enter heaven—one that includes my son and a very beautiful, very special lady," he told her in a low, intense voice.

He took her hand and tucked it into his arm as they continued on their path to his estate.

Katherine had not been sure his words were loud enough to reach her parents behind them, but obviously they had. "Did you hear that, Raven? I believe he was referring to our daughter," her mother whispered to the duke but not low enough to keep everyone from hearing.

Katherine wondered if she'd spend the entire courtship in a constant state of humiliation.

Then again, perhaps it was the least she would deserve.

six

While his servants were preparing the garden for their picnic, Thomas took the opportunity to show the Montbattens around the manor. He was proud of the large estate that had been in his mother's family for three hundred years. His late wife, Anne, had started renovations on it, but he had not done anything else to it since his return. He was now glad he had not, since he had an idea of letting Katherine do the honors. But, as it was, Rosehaven was beautiful with its old family paintings and crystal chandeliers.

His pride and joy, however, were the sixteenth-century tapestries that hung in what used to be the great hall of the manor and was now his drawing room. When the workers had begun cleaning the attics, they'd found the pieces of art still intact and well preserved.

"It is wonderful how they could depict the various aspects of their lives with only a needle and thread," Katherine commented, as she studied one of the larger tapestries about the large room. He'd been thrilled to learn she was interested in history as much as he.

"I don't see what all this fuss is about. They're just musty old cloths with funny-looking pictures nobody cares about. Didn't they have anything else to do with their time?" Lucy plopped down on one of the cushioned chairs in the center of the room, a bored expression clearly marked on her pert features.

"Lucy, if you'd turn your attentions to acting more like a lady, you'd know all accomplished ladies do needlework, play the pianoforte, and follow all manner of other pursuits," Lady

Montbatten said. "Take your sister for an example. She does some of the finest needlework I've ever seen."

Upon hearing more praise about her older sibling, Lucy threw back her head and groaned. It was all Thomas could do not to laugh at her antics, but he contained himself when he saw the frown of disapproval Katherine shot her sister.

"Mother, you cannot compare my little needlework to these great works of art. It is like comparing apples to oranges."

"Speaking of fruit," Thomas said when he saw his butler, McInnes, nod at him from the doorway, "I believe our luncheon is ready for us in the garden. Shall we?"

Thomas offered his arm to Katherine, and with Lucy trailing behind them, they followed the duke and duchess out into the garden. Before they reached their table, Thomas took the opportunity to whisper to Katherine, "After we dine, perhaps you'd like to see my stables. I have been told you are a great admirer of Arabians, and I've just purchased two."

Katherine's eyes lit up, causing Thomas's insides to do a strange little flip-flop. "I would, indeed, like to see them!"

"Me, too!" Lucy broke in. "I absolutely love horses!"

Katherine and Thomas glanced back to find the girl imploring them with hopeful eyes. Thomas then shared a helpless look with Katherine. "Of course, you may come, too."

"She is quite the clever girl, isn't she?" Thomas whispered with a chuckle once they'd continued to walk in the garden.

"If you want to call being a troublemaker and eavesdropper clever," Katherine returned with a sigh. "I keep waiting for her to grow up and out of her directness and become more ladylike. I fear I shall not survive it if she does not do it soon!"

Thomas shrugged. "When you are living apart from her, you will be able to appreciate her more."

"When would I—?" Katherine froze in midsentence.

Thomas smiled, thinking she must have contented herself

with the notion she would probably never leave her parents before he came along. "When you marry, of course," he finished smoothly, giving her a significant glance.

He watched her blush and look away.

North was already waiting for them, as well as Mrs. Sanborne with Ty. Theodora, Thomas noticed with dissatisfaction, had also returned. An uneasiness stirred inside him. He still had not figured out how much influence the woman, who appeared to be in her mid-thirties, had on Katherine. But something was there, for Katherine was constantly looking to her cousin when she was around.

As she was doing now, he observed. The minute she realized Theodora was present, she left his side and went to greet her. They shared a few whispers between them, and Theodora seemed to be arguing with Katherine about something. She was frowning at first, but when he started toward her to direct her to her seat, she was all smiles.

"Is everything all right?" he asked in a low voice as he held out her chair.

"Of course!" she exclaimed, her expression questioning.

He stared at her a moment, trying to see behind the façade she'd suddenly put on, but he could decipher nothing. With a silent sigh, he gave her a small smile and went to his seat at the head of the table, where she sat on his right and her mother on his left. Theodora was seated well away from them—he made sure of it.

As they partook of the delicious chicken his cook had prepared, conversation flowed easily between Thomas, North, and the elder Montbattens. Katherine was noticeably quiet during the meal, a problem Thomas hoped to question her about once they were at the stables later.

At one point, his son became cranky as he usually did around his noon naptime, but when Mrs. Sanborne got up to take him inside the manor, Katherine surprised him by stopping her and asking if she could hold him for a while.

Thomas tried to pay attention to the conversations around him after that, but his gaze was drawn to the interaction between Katherine and Ty. He'd immediately quieted when she took him, and as she carried him about the garden, singing softly to him, he'd slowly begun to nod off. He was surprised she could handle carrying him about like that, since he was over a year now and getting fairly heavy. After that, she'd settled on one of the iron benches and leaned back so the toddler was straddling her waist with his chubby legs and resting his head under her chin.

The sight of them made his heart yearn for her to be his wife and mother to his son. This would be a familiar sight, one that would extend to other children they would have.

And she would be his. He would be able to reach out to her as he wanted to, wrapping his arms around her, holding her to his heart, knowing she would be his wife and love forever.

God knew he wanted that more than anything.

"Isn't that right, Lord Thomas?" Lucy's voice jarred Thomas out of his reverie. He glanced around to find everyone at the table staring at him.

"Isn't what right, Lucy?"

Thomas had the eerie feeling the young girl knew exactly what had been on his mind. "The horses. Were not you going to show me your prized Arabians?" she asked, apparently for the second time.

"Oh! Yes, of course." He glanced about the table. "I promised Lucy and Katherine I would show them my horses I have just recently acquired. Would anyone else like to join us?"

The duke shook his head. "Not I. I fancy sitting here in the shade a bit and resting after such a fine meal." He nodded toward his wife. "You may go, my dear, if you would like."

Lady Montbatten smiled. "Oh, no. I'll join my husband in his rest." She turned to her youngest daughter. "You should rest also, Lucy. Why not let Theodora go in your place?"

Before Lucy could voice her protest, Thomas intervened. "Both ladies are welcome to join me." He sent his friend a pointed look. "You will come also, North?"

North must have understood he needed him along for distraction. "Indeed. But I warn you, if I spend too much time admiring them, you might find some of them missing when I am gone!" he teased.

Everyone laughed, and Thomas took the opportunity to walk to where Katherine was holding Ty. "Why don't you let Mrs. Sanborne take him now and put him to bed? I would imagine he is growing quite heavy for you."

Katherine nodded and slowly stood up with the sleeping child. Mrs. Sanborne took him from her, and Thomas noticed a bittersweet smile on Katherine's lips as she watched them go into the manor. "I believe my son is quite enamored of you," Thomas told her, bringing her gaze back to him.

She grinned up at him. "As I am he. Tyler is a fine little boy, Thomas. You seem to be doing well with him."

Thomas nodded thoughtfully, debating whether to say his next words. He decided it would not hurt to start hinting around at his feelings. "I suppose I do well enough, but it doesn't follow we are content in our situation." She merely seemed curious, so he continued. "Every little boy should have a mother."

At those words, Katherine turned away, and he was unable to read her reaction.

"May we go now?" Lucy asked impatiently then.

Thomas sighed inwardly and watched Katherine use the interruption as an excuse to walk away from him. "Yes, of course." He walked toward the group and noticed Theodora was now talking to Katherine. Confused again at her odd behavior, he held out his hand to Lucy, then motioned his head to North to join him.

As the men and Lucy took the lead down the path that led to the stables, Katherine and Theodora hung back a ways, still whispering in what sounded like an argument.

"Lucy," Thomas said in a low voice, "I was wondering if you might help me in a plan that involves your sister and Miss Vine."

Lucy, just as Thomas had supposed, grew excited by the idea of conspiring against her sister. "Oh, I would! What did you have in mind?" she whispered back, her voice full of excitement.

Thomas exchanged a glance with North. "I need you and North to distract Theodora so I might speak with your sister alone. It would be only for a few minutes."

Lucy's eyes narrowed on Thomas, and a conspiratorial smile curved her lips. "You like my sister, do you not?"

Thomas smothered his chuckle with a choked cough. "Uh—yes, I do."

She nodded with wisdom beyond her years. "And I suppose you want to be alone with her to recite sonnets or some other such romantic gesture."

North was the one choking back a laugh this time. "Do you have your sonnets on hand, Thom?"

Thomas chuckled. "Perhaps I shall save the sonnets for another day. Today I only want to talk to her."

"All right," she said with resignation, though by her tone, Thomas understood the girl thought her idea of sonnets a better plan than his.

They had arrived at the stables, so Thomas ushered them inside. As usual, the large building was kept clean and tidy.

"It smells in here," Theodora was quick to comment.

"It *is* a stable, Theo," Lucy retorted.

"Do not call me that, Lucinda!" her cousin snapped back in a low, menacing voice.

Thomas saw Lucy was about to say something back, and he jumped in hastily. "North, why don't you escort Theodora and Lucy outside where the air is fresher."

North nodded, giving Theodora one of his charming smiles. "Excellent idea!" He held out his arm to the woman. "Shall we?"

Thomas was interested to see the older woman actually start to blush and preen a bit. "I would love to," she said softly, but then she suddenly remembered her duty. "But Kate will be without a chaperone."

"We will only be right outside. I am sure her reputation will be safe with that and all the groomsmen about," North countered smoothly.

That was all the convincing it took. North had so enthralled the woman with his appeal, she would have probably followed the handsome duke anywhere. So with Lucy on his other arm, they left Thomas alone with Katherine.

Finally.

ða

Katherine watched her cousin with astonishment as she walked out of the stables hanging on to the Duke of Northingshire's arm and gazing at him with adoring eyes.

Where has the spinsterish woman gone who is always quoting platitudes on why women are better off without men? she wondered.

"Ah! Here we are." Thomas brought her attention to the horse he was standing beside. "This beauty is named Sultan, and though he is a lot to handle, he can run like the wind. Come—you can pet him. He's like most males who become big babies when a lovely lady is around."

The sleek black horse was, indeed, beautiful, and with a little reverence, Katherine reached out and ran her hand down his forehead and nose. The horse, just as Thomas had predicted, moved to snuggle his head more into her hand. "Oh! You are a big baby, are you not?" she crooned.

Katherine looked up to find Thomas studying her. She became disconcerted because it seemed he could see so deeply into her heart and mind, discerning her secrets. She lowered her eyes. "Why do you stare at me so?"

Thomas turned away, and he, too, began stroking the horse's mane. "I suppose I am trying to understand you," he commented evenly, but Katherine could tell it was a subject that was serious to him.

She did not want to speak of serious things with Thomas. Serious talk would lead to serious questions such as those concerning marriage. And as much as Theodora was urging her to hint around about the subject, she was experiencing much anxiety about doing so.

"There is nothing to understand," she countered with a shrug, walking over to the horse in the next stall.

"Sometimes you seem very comfortable in my presence, then in an instant you become uncomfortable." His voice was low and full of confusion and concern as he came up behind her.

Katherine closed her eyes, fighting off feelings that would only complicate the already horrible situation. "I—I don't know what you're talking about. I—"

"Is it because of my brother? Do I remind you of him, and that is what makes you become distant?" he interrupted her, then placed his hands on her shoulders and gently turned her to face him. "Do you love him still?"

Katherine felt the warmth of his hands linger on her shoulders, and part of her wished she could step a few inches more into his arms. Somehow she knew his strong arms would make her feel safe—that everything would make sense.

She looked fully into those deep blue eyes that were so much like his brother's yet filled with a love and respect she had never seen in Nicholas's, and she knew she'd never been in love with his elder sibling. Neither had he been in love with her. They'd had an arrangement, one that benefited them, their families, and their station. She wanted revenge against him, not because she'd been scorned by love but because she had been so humiliated over the aftermath of the breakup.

And she was going to make Thomas pay for a humiliation he had nothing to do with? It made no sense now. Not when she was staring into the eyes of a man whose honor and integrity showed so clearly there.

What a wicked person she was. Would God ever forgive her for what she had planned to do?

"I am not in love with Nicholas, Thomas," she told him honestly, and it hurt her physically to see his eyes light up with relief. "And though you resemble each other, there is not much about you that reminds me of him. To be honest, we never really talked much, and I saw him as rather arrogant and self-seeking, whereas you are unpretentious and very giving."

His smile grew at her words, and Katherine knew he was pleased. "I am glad you do not compare us and that your heart is not tied to him." He stopped for a moment, then continued hesitantly. "But I do want you to know he is not the same man he was. I can honestly say God has wrought a great change in his life. I do not think you would recognize him as he is today." He smiled teasingly. "Although he can still be a little arrogant. But I believe being the Earl of Kenswick brings that on ever so often."

A wave of resentment shot through her as Thomas spoke of the changes in his brother. It seemed unfair for Nicholas to be so much in God's favor when she felt as though God had forgotten her. And with the terrible thoughts she'd had and the dastardly plans she had made, she would probably never feel His favor again. "I have also changed, but I sometimes think it is not for the better and that God has had little to do with it," she found herself admitting, surprising them both.

Thomas frowned and moved to take her hands into his own. "You are wrong, Katherine. God can take any bad situation and turn it around for good. Of course, you know what He did for me! Coming that close to death made me realize how much I needed God and how much I should cherish the people in my life. I hated going through it, but now that I am on the other side, I can see God's plan." He caressed the back of her bare hands. "Now that we have met, can you not see how everything can turn out to be better than either of us ever dreamed?"

Katherine wanted to turn and run away from him and his eyes full of adoration. His words were like someone putting bricks upon her shoulders, weighing her down with even more guilt and shame. Why didn't she turn to God when the rumors had started? Why had she allowed bitterness to choke out her happiness and peace?

But she couldn't run. She was caught in a web of her own making—one she didn't know how to get out of.

"Yes, of course I can," she murmured, hating herself for being such a coward and not confessing the whole truth to him.

"Look—why don't you come to the manor tomorrow? Nicholas and his wife, Christina, should be arriving at noon. I think it would help you to talk to him after all this time. I know he has some apologies he would like to make to you personally."

"Oh, no," she answered quickly, knowing she was not ready to face Nicholas. Not yet. Maybe not ever, if she could not find a way of backing out of the plan. "I'm sorry, Thomas, but I just can't."

Thomas seemed disappointed, but he tried to hide it. "It is all right, Katherine," he said. "There will be other times. And when the time is right, I will be with you."

Katherine squeezed his hand and smiled at him, although she felt like crying.

seven

Thomas waited until his brother and sister-in-law had reunited with Ty before he told them of his involvement with Katherine. Because they had both raised his son the first few months of his life, when everyone had presumed he was dead, Thomas did not want his news to upset them right away.

As Christina and Nicholas played with the toddler and chatted with him, Thomas could see they were very happy in their marriage. Nicholas, though always retaining his regal bearing, was a more considerate person now, friendlier, with a ready smile, than he had been after their father had died.

The more Thomas talked with them, the more he began to think that maybe his news would not bother his brother at all. Perhaps he would even be happy for him!

"By the way"—he decided to go for the nonchalant approach—"Katherine and her family are at their castle for the season."

Thomas saw Nicholas turn to gauge Christina's expression as if to see her reaction to his old fiancée's name. When she merely smiled at him and continued to play with her nephew, Nicholas responded. "Indeed. I am surprised they are not in London this time of year. The London season was always an event of great importance to the duke and duchess." His voice was calm, and, in fact, he didn't seem interested in pursuing the subject, giving Thomas even more confidence in what he needed to say.

"Yes, well, I believe the Montbattens felt their stay in the country was more beneficial than attending the season."

When he received no response from his brother, who had reached for the baby and was now holding him up in the air, he became more specific. "More beneficial to Katherine."

Nicholas froze, then slowly lowered the baby, keeping his razor sharp gaze trained on his nervous brother. "Are you trying to tell me Katherine has a suitor?" Then to Thomas's amazement, he laughed. "And you thought this would bother me?"

Thomas cleared his throat. "Well, yes, but—"

"Thom, this is the best news I've heard all day! Do you know how guilty I've felt knowing Katherine's name was so blackened over our engagement that she's had no offers? This brings a sort of closure to that whole dreadful episode in our lives!"

"Tell us, Thomas! Who is he?" Christina piped up as she ran to sit on the sofa next to him. It amazed him to think this beautiful redhead had been the vicar's little daughter who gave them so much grief when they were younger. She still had that unchanging spark shining in her eyes and the impish grin he remembered so well. It was her hope and faith that had refused to give up on his brother, even when Nicholas tried to shut her and everyone else out of his life after the war.

"Yes, tell us! Do you know him?" Nicholas seconded.

Thomas took a deep breath. "Yes, and you know him, too. I am Katherine's suitor."

There was a moment of stunned silence as both Nicholas and Christina stared at him, but then his brother leaned his head back and roared with laughter. "You?" He laughed some more. "That is good, Thom. You have developed quite a keen wit since your return from sea."

Thomas looked helplessly from Nicholas to Christina, then he noticed she did not share her husband's laughter. "I do not think it is a joke, Nicholas," she said to him, but her eyes were studying her brother-in-law.

Nicholas wiped the tears of laughter from his eyes with one arm as the other rolled a ball to Ty, who was sitting in front of him. "Of course he is, Christina. If you knew Katherine, you would understand the two of them would be a mix-match if ever there were one! Tell her, Thom. Tell her you are only joking!"

Thomas pulled his gaze from Christina and settled on his brother. It didn't take long for the mirth to fade from Nicholas's face. "You can't be serious!" he charged, his low voice incredulous.

"I have never been more serious, Nick. I am soon going to ask for her hand, and I believe she will accept."

Nicholas picked up the baby, stood, and placed him in Christina's arms. He then turned and grabbed Thomas by his lapels and yanked him up to stand in front of him. "Have you gone completely mad? You cannot marry that woman. She is all wrong for you!" He gave him a hard shake. "You deserve someone better than a society girl for you and for Ty!" At those derogatory words toward Katherine, Thomas got angry and pushed his brother away. "Katherine has changed as much as you have, Nick. How could she not after all she has been through?" he roared at him. "And I do not believe Tyler could have a better mother than Katherine, either, so I will not have you malign her character when you do not know the truth."

Nicholas was not stirred by his loyal speech. He stepped closer to his brother and ignored his wife's plea to calm down. "I was engaged to the woman, you idiot! I probably know her better than you do, so don't paint a pretty picture of a matronly paragon when I know her for who she is!"

The brothers were practically nose to nose now and breathing heavily. Thomas thought if he could just get in one good punch, it certainly would make him feel better.

"What does that say about you if you think of her as unmarriageable? You were only weeks away from marrying her yourself!"

Nicholas snarled. "I was marrying her because of her position, Brother, the exact reason she was marrying me! We were a social match, nothing more!" He poked Thomas in the chest, causing Thomas to ball his fist. "She's using you, Thom, because no one else will have her!"

"You are wrong!" Thomas stated emphatically.

"I wish I were, but I fear I am not!"

"Would you look at yourselves?" All sweetness was gone from Christina's voice, and a steeliness was in its place. "What a fine example you are setting for Tyler!"

The brothers did not back away from each other, but they did glance in her direction—both of their faces swathed in hostility.

Christina shook her head with a snort of disgust. "Just try not to kill him, will you, Thom?" she snapped as she started toward the door with Tyler sitting on her hip. "His baby will need a father, too!"

Both men started as she slammed the large door behind her, but Thomas wasn't sure it was from the sound or the news she'd dropped at their feet.

"Did she say baby?" Nicholas asked, staring back at his brother.

Thomas nodded. "I think she did."

Suddenly, Thomas was swallowed in his brother's joyful embrace. "I'm going to be a father! Did you hear that, Thom? We're having a baby!"

"I heard it—I heard. Now can you please—cease—pounding my back!" Thomas gasped and took a deep breath when he was finally released.

Nicholas shook his finger at his brother. "This conversation is not over with, Thom. I will not stand for you throwing your life away on someone who doesn't truly love you!"

Thomas was quickly regaining his anger. "She does care for me, and I will find a way to prove it to you!" he shot back, knocking Nicholas's hand away. "As a matter of fact, I'm going to Ravenhurst to propose right now!"

He stomped to the door, determined to see it through.

"You are making a mistake, Thom! Just wait until—" Nicholas tried to reason, following him to the door.

"Go to your wife, Nick. You know—the wife that all society thought you should not marry because she was not of our class!" he countered.

"You will regret—" Nicholas began to threaten. Thom walked out of the room, however, ignoring his brother's roar of anger, and slammed the door of the manor behind him.

⁂

"I have been searching for you all morning!" Theodora announced in a peeved tone as she stepped carefully down the steep incline to where Katherine sat on the ground with her book. Usually no one thought to seek her out in the grassy ditch that had once been the castle's moat long years ago. That could only mean her cousin was determined to converse with her.

Not bothering to hide her sigh, she lowered her book of poetry and waited for Theodora to reach her. "Was there something important you wanted?" she asked, though she knew what the answer was.

"Of course I have something important I need to discuss with you, and you are quite aware of it!" Theodora snapped. She sat opposite Katherine, clearly uncomfortable on the uneven surface. "I want to know why you did not accept Thomas's invitation to meet his brother today? Proving to him his brother matters little to you would be all he'd need to ask for your hand!"

"How did you know about that? Were you eavesdropping?"

Theodora stuck up her chin with a defiant air. "No, but Lucy was, then she told me."

Katherine closed her eyes and shook her head tiredly. "I cannot face Nicholas. Not yet."

"You do not want to face him because then you will remember the reason you need to take revenge." She shook her finger at the younger woman. "You are beginning to like him, aren't you? You are allowing yourself to be taken in by yet another Thornton!"

Katherine licked her bottom lip as she gathered up courage for what she needed to say. "There may be truth in what you are saying, Dora," she admitted. "I just know he is too good a person to hurt the way we had planned."

"Not this again!" Theodora threw her arms up in disgust. "I never realized you were such a coward, Kate!"

"It is not cowardly to want to avoid hurting someone, Dora. Thomas is not his brother. He would never break an engagement and leave me to suffer society's rumors for it! He is more honorable than that!"

Katherine could tell Theodora was not at all happy with what she was saying. "What if he knew what his brother had planned all along?" she asked finally, her eyes becoming shrewd as she pinned them on Katherine. "He left for sea right after Nicholas broke your engagement. How do you know Thomas did not encourage his brother in this pursuit because he wanted you for himself!"

Katherine gasped. "You are mad to think such a thing! I will not hear such awful allegations—"

"Don't you think it a coincidence that the first woman he decides to court after his time of mourning is you, when there are many other women he could have pursued."

Katherine covered her ears. "I will not listen. He was a married man then!"

Theodora pushed herself closer to her cousin and pulled her

hands away. "I am simply trying to open your mind to the reality of who the Thorntons are! They are brothers, Katherine, cut from the same cloth!"

Theodora's words did not achieve what she had hoped. Katherine knew in her heart Thomas was a good man; she could see it in his eyes, feel it in his words. "Thomas has told me his brother had a difficult time following the war, and that is why—"

"Do you hear yourself? Now you are defending the man who made you the scourge of all society!" Theodora all but screeched as she jumped up, waving her arm about to emphasize her words.

"I'm not. I—"

"Yes, you are!" Theodora interrupted. "Are you going to let Lord Nicholas Thornton get away with what he did to you? Are you going to let him live an unscathed life with his wife and future children while you wither away as an old maid? Must he live a happy life while you suffer?"

It occurred to Katherine she would still live as an old maid even if she did go along with the plan.

But you could be happily wed if you forget the plan and decide to marry Thomas instead, a little voice sounded in her head. A voice Katherine wanted so much to follow but was afraid to.

"I need time to think," she cried softly as she arose from the ground and dusted the grass from her cream-colored morning dress.

"My lady!" a voice called from atop the ditch by the castle wall, and Katherine squinted up through the bright sunlight to see her maid looking down at her.

"Yes, Stevens, what is it?" she inquired, glad for the interruption.

"His grace has asked to see you in his study," she explained, but then added, "Lord Thornton is with him, also."

"He has done it! He has come to ask for your hand!"

Theodora crowed with delight, not caring that the servant was hearing every word.

Katherine hastily dismissed the girl. "Tell my father I will be right up."

When she'd gone, Katherine glared at Theodora. "If you speak of such things in front of the servants, it will cause more gossip! Lord Thomas could be here to see Cameron, not ask for my hand!"

"Cameron is in town, so I do not think that is the reason," Theodora countered, then added, "I have one caution to make before you speak with him, Cousin."

Katherine let out a breath of impatience. "What is that, Dora?"

"If you are thinking of forgetting our plan, I would advise that you don't." Her lips curved in a false smile. "Nothing stays secret forever. One day Thomas could find out the truth of what we were going to do, and the result will be the same. He will be devastated, and the whole Thornton family will be affected by it."

The impact of what Theodora was saying took her breath away. "Are you making a threat, Dora?"

Her cousin's face was blank. "Of course not, Kate. I'm surprised you would have to ask!"

But it was a threat, and Katherine knew it. What she couldn't figure out was why Theodora was so adamant they proceed with the plan. Why was the Thorntons' ruin so important to her?

Shaken and suddenly afraid, she turned and made her way carefully up the steep incline, for the first time in a long while praying as she went. She prayed with all her heart Theodora could not turn against her but feared that, given the right circumstances, she would.

eight

The moment Katherine walked into the castle, her mother was there, grabbing her by the arm and all but dragging her to her father's study. Though she was talking erratically and too excitedly for Katherine to understand every word, she did hear something about dresses, flowers, and posting banns. That was all she needed to hear.

Apparently, Theodora was right.

"Mama, please!" she protested, making her mother come to a stop. "Let me take a moment to catch my breath."

"Now you must listen to me, Katherine." Her mother took both her shoulders in her hands, gripping firmly. "You are to say yes, do you understand me? Do not do anything to make this fine gentleman change his mind."

Katherine once again felt the pressure of what she was about to do. "Perhaps he is not the man for me, Mama. Perhaps he is not what he seems. Should I risk being shamed for a second time?" she asked, her words spoken out of panic.

"He is just a man, Katherine, and, of course, he probably has his faults, but that is not the point." She let go of her daughter's shoulders and folded her arms across her chest, giving her a stern look. "If you marry him, then it will dispel the ugly rumors, and we can once again mingle in polite society unencumbered. As is our right, Katherine." She whipped a handkerchief out of her pocket and began dabbing at her face. "As is our right!" she whispered fervently, almost as if she were trying to speak it into existence.

Katherine was even too nervous to be bothered by her

mother's histrionics. All she could think about was how angry her parents would be if she followed through with the plan. She knew it might even backfire on them and further lower them in society's eyes.

"Well, don't stand there, Katherine. Go in! Your father and Lord Thomas are waiting for you!" her mother urged in a shrill voice, pushing her toward the door.

Katherine managed to open the door and enter without stumbling, and as expected, there Thomas stood with her father, laughing together as if they were already old friends.

"Ah! Katherine, you are here finally." Her father spoke first. He motioned for her to come closer. "I believe Lord Thornton has something he would like to speak to you about." He shifted his broad grin and shining gaze between them both. "I will leave you two alone."

"Papa!" Katherine called out to him in alarm. "I don't mind if you stay!"

Immediately after the words were out of her mouth, she felt foolish for saying them. Thomas was staring at her with a frown, and her father appeared as though he wanted to strangle her. He didn't say a word to her, either. He merely backed out of the room, closing the door soundly behind him.

"Are you all right, Katherine?" Thomas asked, his voice hesitant.

It hurt to see Thomas standing there dressed so handsomely in his dark brown coat, buckskins, and Hessians— boots that were kept in the finest polish she'd ever beheld.

"Are you going to look at me or just stare at my feet all morning?"

Her head popped up, and she felt her face grow hot. "I'm sorry. I am a bit distracted this morning." She scanned the room, then motioned toward two chairs that stood in front of her father's heavy oak desk. "Did you want to sit down?"

Thomas smiled at her as he took a step closer. "I do believe you are nervous, Katherine." He took her hand and kissed her knuckles. "I do not think it would be hard to guess why I am here."

Katherine took a moment to regain her wits after his gentle kiss. If kissing her hand made her heart beat so fast, what would a true kiss do to her?

"Uh—yes, I think I do know," she answered after a moment. "What are you doing?" she asked when he sank down to one knee, still holding her hand.

He smiled sweetly at her. "I am kneeling before you, my dear Katherine, offering you my heart and my name if you will have them."

Katherine could not help the tears that filled her eyes. She wanted nothing more than to accept his proposal and admit she loved him in return. But with Dora's threat playing in her mind, she was torn about what she should do. "I–I, uh. . . ," she stammered.

When an answer was not forthcoming, the smile left his face and was replaced by an air of trepidation. "Katherine?" He stood up slowly. "Have I misread your feelings for me?"

"No!" she found herself crying out. "I mean—"

"I know what you mean," he interrupted her with a jubilant grin. "It must be that I have proceeded so suddenly—"

"Yes!" She grabbed on to his excuse. "We have known one another for such a short time! Perhaps we should get to know one another better."

Thomas laughed at that statement and brought her hand to his mouth once again. "You are anxious!" he surmised. "Don't be, my lady. We will have a wonderful life together, and I promise you'll never have to endure being snubbed at a party or have your name bandied about in degrading terms. Not as long as I am there to protect and defend you."

After that touching speech, Katherine knew no woman alive would respond differently than she. "I'll marry you."

He became still, her hand still safely enfolded in his own. "You will?"

She took a breath, tried not to think about what would happen in the future, and nodded. And perhaps she wanted to do a little pretending, too.

"Katherine," he murmured, his eyes full of emotion as he drew her to him. Her eyes grew large as she realized he intended to kiss her.

"Kath—!" Her sister barged through the door and froze when she saw them in a semi-embrace. "Aha! I've caught you again, and this time I do not think he was aiming for your hand!" she charged loudly, her eyes full of curiosity.

"Lucinda! What are you doing in there?" her mother's voice echoed from the hallway, then she, too, was standing there staring at the couple.

Thomas had already stepped away from her but was still holding her hand.

Her father appeared; both parents looked back and forth to try to gauge the couple's demeanor. "Might we deduce that by your holding hands there is to be a wedding in the near future?" Katherine's mother asked carefully.

"Indeed, there is!" Thomas answered with elation.

"Capital!" her father exclaimed, stepping forward to shake hands with him and give Katherine a kiss on the cheek.

Her mother's reaction was, of course, more dramatic. "Ooh!" she cried. Large tears formed in her eyes. Waving her hand-kerchief about, Lady Montbatten hurried over to Thomas, put her hands on either side of his face, and whispered emotionally with a properly shaking voice, "Welcome to the family, Thomas. And please call me Mama!"

Thomas had a bemused expression on his face as she kissed each cheek, then clutched her handkerchief to her mouth as if to hold off a sob. She then moved on to Katherine to give her a hug.

Of course, no one but she heard her mother whisper, "Excellent, dear. You have saved us all!"

❧

Thomas stayed at Ravenhurst Castle for a little while longer as the family talked excitedly of their engagement. Even Theodora had seemed excited about it and kept giving Katherine a strange smile, almost as if she were communicating her approval of the event.

Something about Katherine's older cousin bothered him greatly, but he could not put a finger on why. He seemed to remember knowing her several years ago, but he could not remember in what circumstance. He thought it might have been in the village of Malbury where he grew up, but he couldn't be certain. Obviously, it had not been a memorable meeting, and she *was* several years older than his twenty-seven.

Once he reached his home, Thomas took a few minutes to think about what to say to his brother. He had rushed to the castle in haste and out of anger, but he could not be sorry he had asked Katherine to marry him. His argument with his brother only hastened him to do what he desired to do in the first place.

He was to marry Katherine Montbatten, the woman he truly loved with all his heart.

If his brother could not accept it, then that would be something left for Nicholas to deal with. His brother had found true love and happiness; now Thomas had, also.

But surely his brother would come to accept his choice. They were both Christian men, and they knew God put people in their lives according to His will and not the dictates of men.

"Are you going to stand out here all day, or have you gathered enough courage yet to face me?" Nicholas spoke from behind Thomas, startling him.

"It's not courage I am gathering, Brother," he countered.

"I'm trying to remember my defensive training from the war in case you decide to try a hit at me."

Nicholas chuckled while shaking his head. "I suppose you've gone and done the deed, haven't you?" he said, getting to the point of the matter.

Thomas lifted his chin. "I have." The two men stared at one another. "Will this drive a wedge between us, Nick?"

Nicholas glanced away for a moment, and when he looked back, Thomas saw the emotion he was fighting hard to hide. "I suffered for a year thinking my only brother had been taken from me. Do you honestly believe I would allow anyone—even an ex-fiancée—to drive a wedge between us?"

Thomas was blinking back tears of his own as he and Nicholas embraced. Then with a hearty slap on the back, Nicholas declared, "Come! We must go and tell Tyler he will soon gain not only a new mother but a new cousin as well!"

Thomas's eyes widened. "Then it is true? I am to be an uncle?"

Nicholas nodded proudly. "Yes, and this time I will not hire a nanny who repeats the same word with every sentence! I was almost driven mad when Mrs. Sanborne was living at Kenswick!"

Thomas laughed and led his brother into the manor. "I think she is quite endearing."

Nicholas snorted. "Why does that not surprise me?"

⁂

"What are you doing back down in the moat?" Theodora called from above. Katherine squinted up from her seat on the ground where she had been trying to sort out her feelings—in peace.

"I am trying to think, if you do not mind," Katherine returned waspishly, not caring whether or not it angered Theodora.

"But I do mind!" Katherine turned in time to observe

Theodora stumbling down the incline again—invading her sanctuary. "We must discuss where to go next with our plan."

Katherine drew her knees up and buried her head in her folded arms. "I do not want to discuss it. Not now!"

"Yes, now!" her cousin's shrill voice demanded. "Cameron has returned from town, and it is the perfect opportunity!"

Katherine's head snapped up. "What does Cameron have to do with this?"

Theodora smiled as she peered down at her. "He is the second part of our plan, dear Cousin. Cameron will not be happy about your engagement since he truly hates all the Thorntons for what they did to you."

"What *he* did, Dora. Nicholas. He's the only one who hurt me," she corrected.

"That is neither here nor there, Kate. What matters is that Cameron is bound to stir up trouble. He's already issued two challenges to the earl. He was humiliated by his not accepting, so I would wager he will turn his anger toward Lord Thomas."

Katherine stared at her cousin with horror. "Are you hoping Cameron will shoot Thomas in a duel?"

Theodora laughed. "Of course I am not saying that." She shrugged. "But if one does occur. . ." She let her sentence drift off to be left to Katherine's imagination.

Katherine jumped up with her hands on her hips. "And what if it is Cameron who is shot or even killed?"

"Perhaps they'll choose swords! You know how good Cameron is with those!"

Katherine began to walk away from Theodora, back up the steep hill. "Your words are evil ones, Cousin, and I will listen no longer."

Theodora was clambering to keep up, but she'd gone only a few steps before she tripped and rolled a short way back down the incline. "Aren't you going to help me?" she screeched when Katherine glanced back but kept on walking.

Katherine did not answer her, so upset was she over Theodora's callous attitude. In fact, she didn't even see Cameron until she collided into him.

"Oh! I did not know you were there!" Katherine gasped as she grabbed onto his strong arms.

Cameron smiled fondly at his sister as he helped her gain her balance. "I am afraid I was preoccupied myself, wondering what all the screaming coming from the moat was about."

Katherine sighed, feeling a little guilty. "Theodora fell partway down the ditch, and I was so angry at her that I did not stop to help her."

"I do not know why you put up with her at all, Kate. I've never met anyone quite so unpleasant as she!"

Katherine stared up at her brother, who was two years older than she and whom she had always admired. He was a big man, muscular from working with his horses and fencing, and so very handsome with his curly golden hair and light green eyes. From her earliest memories, she saw Cameron as her protector, someone who was kind and gentle with her but would fight to the death if anyone or anything tried to harm her.

That was why she was so terrified to tell him about the engagement. She had no idea of what his reaction would be.

"Theodora has no one else, Cameron—you know that. I fail to notice her undesirable qualities, I suppose," she said in response to his comment.

"You are a far better person than I, Kate," he said with a grin as he tucked her hand into his arm and began escorting her to the castle. "Now tell me—what is all the excitement about around here? The servants are running about like mad whispering, and neither Papa nor Mama has time to answer when I ask. They all refer me to you. So what is going on?"

"I have become engaged, Cameron," she said quickly.

"That is wonder—"

"Stop!" she interrupted with a cry, halting their walk. "First let me tell you who the man is."

"Kate, do not be so anxious. I know I am protective of you, but I promise I will accept anyone who has broken with the attitudes of the *ton* and has chosen to pursue you," he tried to assure her.

"Remember you promised, Cameron, for the man is Lord Thomas Thornton."

It was as if a thundercloud came and sat upon her brother's head. "Surely you cannot be that stupid!" he roared, shaking her hand from his arm and glaring at her as if she were poison. "The Thorntons are our enemies! What can you be thinking?"

Kate tried to reach out to her brother, but he backed away from her. "Please, Cameron, Thomas is not like his brother. He—"

"Kate, has it become this desperate?" he asked in a calmer voice, as he appeared to be trying to fight his anger. "Do you believe Thornton is the only man who will ask for your hand?"

Kate's eyes filled with tears at seeing her brother's disappointment. "It is not like that, Cameron."

"Then how is it?" Cameron charged but turned away, as if trying to collect his thoughts. "If I had known this earlier, then I would deal with it, but now I cannot. I have to finish out the semester." He pointed his finger at her sternly. "But I will see to this matter, Kate. Do not get married before I return!"

If her brother only knew about the plan. Katherine contemplated telling him, but because she was beginning to like Thomas, she did not. Perhaps she was holding out for a miracle.

"And how long will you be gone?" she asked faintly.

"Four weeks before the summer break."

Katherine and Cameron separated when they entered the castle, for he had to instruct the servants on his luggage.

What she didn't expect, after he had gone from her sight, was her mother rushing toward her. "Is Cameron in his room?"

Katherine blinked with puzzlement. "Yes, but—"

"Lucy has told me about your conversation!" her mother said in a loud stage whisper.

Katherine gaped in amazement. "That little scamp! Was she eavesdropping on me?"

Her mother waved her handkerchief back and forth, giving Katherine a dismissive glance. "That is inconsequential at the moment, dear! What's important is that we must set the date of the wedding posthaste!"

"What do you mean?" Katherine asked, fearful of the determined gleam in her mother's eyes.

"I mean that we must set the wedding date for the thirteenth of June. It will give us four weeks to plan it!"

Katherine shook her head, feeling herself being sucked deeper and deeper into trouble. "It is too soon, Mama. You must let us have time to know one another!"

"Get to know him after you're married. It is what I did and what my mother before me did. It is simply the way of things, dear," her mother instructed her with a shrug. "And, besides, we have to do this before Cameron arrives and tries to challenge him to a duel."

nine

"Where did North pop off to?" Christina asked the next morning when they were all sitting down for breakfast. She was quite stunning in her light green morning dress that complemented her red hair and bright eyes. Though Thomas could tell she had polished up a bit from when he first met her again at their wedding, after knowing her in his younger days, she still had the ability to say and do the oddest, most unladylike things.

Just the day before, he'd found her in his stables inside Sultan's stall, examining his front leg. She had gotten completely dirty from head to foot and was busy smearing a smelly mixture on his leg. She'd explained later it was a medicine to help heal strained muscles—that his horse had been "standing oddly" were her words.

Despite her unladylike behavior, she was still one of the most unusual and charming women Thomas had ever known. He was glad his brother had pushed aside society's expectations and married the vicar's daughter. She obviously adored him, and Thomas wondered if Katherine would be the same loving wife as his sister-in-law was with his brother.

"North is always jotting here and about visiting his friends before he embarks on his trip to America," Thomas explained. "He tells me he will be stopping by Kenswick Hall in a fortnight or so."

"Excellent," Nicholas stated his approval. "He was a good friend to me during my dark time when Father died and I thought I'd lost you, too. I'm glad he's been here for you, also."

"Indeed," Thomas agreed. "And though I know he was disappointed he could not go to America months ago because of the war still raging, I am glad for myself he's been able to visit us here at Rosehaven and in London."

"I wish he wouldn't go over there!" Christina interjected, surprising both brothers at the irritation that was behind her words. "He needs to stay here in England and find a nice girl to marry!"

Thomas was vexed by her outcry, but when he looked toward Nicholas, he saw his brother was not. "Ah." He nodded sagely. "Still holding out hope for your friend Helen, are you?"

"Who is Helen?" Thomas asked.

Christina bristled and shot her husband a piqued glare. "Helen is my very best friend, and she happens to be in love with North."

"Helen is the daughter of Mr. Rupert Nichols, a very nice gentleman farmer but poor. North knows his obligations. His family has a tradition of marrying either royalty or the highest of noble families; it is what's expected of him," Nicholas gently reminded his wife.

"You did not do what was expected of you! Did he not, Thomas?" She suddenly turned to Thomas, peering at him with expectant eyes.

Thomas looked from Christina to his brother. "I don't think I want to answer that. Nicholas may try to challenge me to a duel or something."

Christina gasped, and Nicholas seemed irritated. "Thomas, you know that was a long time ago! He is a Christian man now," she explained in her husband's defense.

"I was only teasing, Christina," Thomas said, knowing his brother had changed from the angry, bitter man he had been after the war when those duels had taken place. He then said, with a twinkle in his eye, "Besides, while he is good with pistols, I am better with the sword. So you see—it would not be a fair fight either way."

Christina started to say something, but she closed her mouth as suddenly as she had opened it. "You are trying to get me off the subject, are you not?"

Thomas grinned, not feeling the least bit guilty for it. "Yes, did it work?"

"No, and I still—" she started to say when Nicholas broke in.

"Getting back to the subject of marriage, are you still in agreement your engagement should be a long one?" Nicholas gave Thomas a look that only older brothers could get away with. A look that told him since their father was gone, he was the one dispensing guidance, so Thomas should adhere to it.

Thomas didn't require his brother's interference, however. Because of Katherine's inconsistent behavior, he, too, saw the need of waiting a bit to know her better and she, him. "I think I shall suggest we wait for at least four months. Perhaps in that time I can get to know Cameron, too, and bring some sort of mending to relationships with him."

"I think that is wise," Nicholas told him, and Thomas could tell he was still not pleased with the whole situation.

"I hope you will be happy, Thomas, as Nicholas has made me happy. I believe God leads the right person into our lives, and when He does, we know it." She reached across the table and put her hand over his. "Do you know, Thomas? Do you have the feeling God has sent her to you?"

Thomas smiled. "Indeed, I do. Even when she was engaged to Nicholas, I thought she was a special person. And when I met her again, it was as if the whole room darkened and one lone light shone directly from Katherine to me." He squeezed her hand gently. "I know God has sent her to me."

Christina's eyes filled with tears. "Oh, my. That was quite a romantic thing to say, Thomas. You should be a poet." She pulled her hand back and started dabbing at her eyes with her napkin.

Nicholas frowned. "You've said the same thing to me, Christina! It doesn't seem quite as special if you are going to be spreading the sentiment to every poor sap who pours out his heart to you!"

Thomas threw his head back and laughed. "You have never been accused of being romantic! Love must be blind after all," he roared, laughing harder when Nicholas jumped up from his chair and leaned menacingly over the table.

Expecting such a reaction, Thomas was quick to push his chair back and stand away from Nicholas.

"I am a changed man, little brother. Tell him I'm a changed man, Christina," Nicholas ordered in a loud, commanding voice.

"He's a changed man, Thomas," Christina parroted dutifully, but the sincerity of the statement was lost when she, too, started to snicker. "Now sit down, dear, before you do something to make us both liars."

Nicholas dragged his glare away from Thomas to his wife. Suddenly he grinned, letting them know he'd been teasing them both. "I'll sit, but you must promise not to pay him any more compliments," he groused but with a playful gleam in his eyes.

"I promise." She turned and gave Thomas a stern frown. "You sit down, too, Thomas, and behave yourself. I fear I must take back the compliments, but I'm sure you will understand."

"I think I do—" he began to tease as his butler, McInnes, came into the room with a slight cough.

"I beg yer pardon, my laird, but dinna ye sae ye'd be wantin' ta see the *Times* this morn?"

Thomas nodded. "Of course, McInnes. Bring it to me."

The wily Scot who'd been butler at Rosehaven for four

years walked with his usual swagger and dropped the paper beside his employer's toast. "Ye might be wantin' ta look o' page four, my laird," McInnes whispered in his ear, and before Thomas could question him on it, he was out of the room.

"I still don't understand why you have a Scot for a butler. I don't believe they have the proper disposition for such an important duty. Did you know he scolded me yesterday for getting dirt on the rug after my morning ride?" Nicholas told him, clearly irritated by the incident.

"Hmm." Thomas barely heard what his brother was saying since he was so intent on turning to page four. "McInnes seemed quite insistent I read something. . . ." His voice drifted off as he read the small item in the center of the paper. "What are you both doing on the thirteenth of June?" he murmured, a little perplexed and just a little pleased by the turn of events.

Nicholas appeared curious. "Why do you ask? What is on page four that has your butler so interested?"

"The engagement has already been published in the *Times*, and it seems the date is only four weeks away on June thirteenth."

"Who is responsible for this?" Nicholas asked.

Thomas stared at the paper without seeing it as his mind pondered the news. He rubbed his chin thoughtfully, then brought his gaze over to his brother. "I believe I shall pay a visit to Ravenhurst Castle to find out."

❧

"I'm sorry, my lord, but Lady Katherine is unavailable," the Montbattens' butler told Thomas, the same thing he'd been telling him for three days. "Perhaps if you'd like to leave your card or a note?"

Thomas stared at the tall, solemn man and contemplated that the man might possess no personality whatsoever. If

Ambrose, as he was called, had one, he'd surely never shown it to him. He'd been to the castle a few times and had surely known of the engagement, and still he treated Thomas as if he were an ordinary caller.

"What of her parents? Are they at home?" he persisted, tired of whatever game was being played at his expense.

"They are in London, my lord. I believe they left two days ago."

Thomas thought something was significant in that piece of news. "And Miss Vine? Is she available?"

"Yes, she is."

Thomas stood staring at Ambrose, who merely stared back at him, expressionless as usual. "Ambrose," he finally said, his voice strained with ire. "Can you please let me come in to speak with Miss Vine?"

The butler nodded regally. "Of course, my lord." Ambrose backed up from the threshold and motioned Thomas inside.

He had to wait only a few minutes in a small sitting room before Theodora came unhurriedly into the room. It was odd watching the woman because her eyes and her expression and tone did not match. It was as if she were a walking contradiction from what she was saying and what she felt. Thomas had the uncanny feeling that Theodora despised him; yet she always seemed to smile at him, and he knew she urged Katherine his way by her insistent whispers and unsubtle hints.

Why? Why was she anxious for Katherine and him to make a match? What would she gain from it?

Something had to be motivating her, he realized. Perhaps God was leading him to find out or maybe even help the woman. He did not want to judge her, so perhaps if he tried to befriend her, he could understand her more.

The thin woman curtsied, and Thomas nodded his head

respectfully her way. "My lord," she began. "I was surprised you wanted to see me. Is something amiss?"

Thomas watched as she walked to a chair and sat down upon it. It was the largest chair in the room, and when she looked up at him, it appeared as though she were sitting on a throne holding court. Shaking the absurd thought from his mind, he smiled at her, then took the chair next to her. "I came to inquire after Katherine. I've tried to see her but have only been told she is not available. Frankly, Miss Vine, I was wondering if she might be ill or something similar to that."

The woman's lips pursed, and Thomas thought if it were possible, steam would be coming from her ears for how upset she seemed. "I'm afraid I do not understand, my lord. I was under the impression Katherine was riding with you every day since your engagement."

Thomas sat back on his seat, dumbfounded by this information. "I have not seen her since the day I asked her to marry me."

Theodora startled him by quickly standing and walking to the window. He turned in his chair to see what she was doing. "I hope I didn't upset you, Miss Vine. It's just that I'd like to know why Katherine is lying to you about seeing me, then ignoring me when I call."

Thomas saw her bony shoulders lift and go back down in an apparent sigh. Slowly, she turned and faced him, all traces of anger gone from her face. "I believe Katherine must be experiencing pre-wedding jitters, my lord."

That did make sense, but Thomas could not get rid of the feeling there was more to it. "I suppose so, but that would explain only why she has been hiding from me. Why would she lie to you?"

She shrugged as she came and sat back down in the chair.

"I must confess, I have encouraged a relationship between you both all along."

"Did you?" he murmured.

"Yes, because I had heard you were a good man and someone who would disregard the gossip that has been spoken of her."

Thomas nodded. "I appreciate your confidence in me."

For a moment, he thought the woman grimaced, but when he blinked, a pleasant expression was clearly shown on her face. Perhaps he had only. . .imagined it.

"I am on your side, Lord Thornton, and will do everything I can to calm her fears so she will speak to you." She stood, and Thomas deduced their little tête-à-tête was over.

He stood. "I thank you, Miss Vine. I shall call again tomorrow." He started to go, but she stopped him.

"Wait!" He turned, and she motioned toward the window. "The moat—or the ditch, rather. I saw her in there by the rear bridge when I glanced out of the window a few moments ago."

Thomas blinked with bemusement. "I'm sorry—did you say 'moat'?"

Theodora sighed with an expression of long-suffering. "Unfortunately, yes. She likes to go and sit at the bottom and—well—I don't know what she does. Thinks or something."

Thomas smiled at the odd woman. "Excellent. Again you have my thanks."

He didn't wait for a response as he hurried from the castle and walked around until he came to the rear bridge. As Theodora had told him, Katherine was there, lying with her back propped against the incline, staring off in front of her.

He was halfway down when she saw him. "What are you doing here?" she asked in a panicked voice, scrambling to her feet.

"I'm here to find out why you have been avoiding me." Thomas came to stand in front of her. "Are you having regrets?" he added quietly.

Katherine began studying the ground as she folded her arms at her waist in a defensive move. "I don't know what you—"

"Look at me, Katherine!" he demanded softly as he took her arms and brought himself closer to her. "First I find that you or someone has published our wedding date without consulting me, and now you are ignoring me. If you did not want to marry me, why did you set the date for the thirteenth of June?"

"I didn't!" she cried, her expression surprisingly defiant. "My mother did that."

Thomas stared at her for a moment, trying to understand the emotions whirling about in her eyes. "Are you doing this for your mother? Because that is no reason to go into marriage. I—"

"No. I'm not doing this for my mother." She closed her eyes, and when she opened them, she gazed directly into his. "I'm just scared, Thomas. I'm scared of—" She stopped, as if she were unable to find the right words.

Thomas thought he knew the answer. "You're scared I'm going to leave you as Nicholas did."

She frowned and started to say something, then stopped. She chewed at her bottom lip as he waited for her to respond. "I—yes—yes, you are right. I'm scared of being hurt."

Thomas smiled, relieved. "My darling, don't be scared. You must realize I lov—"

"No! Do not say it! Please!" she cried, breaking his hold on her and putting her hands over her mouth in an appearance of fear.

"Katherine, why should I not say it? If it is because you are not sure of your own feelings, then I am content to wait until you can say the words. But there is no reason not to express my own."

She was the picture of misery, staring back at him with a stark expression that tore at his heart. "I do have feelings for you, Thomas. I am just afraid, as you said."

"My sweet Katherine," he called out softly, closing the space between them again. "I would not have asked you to marry me if I believed otherwise."

They stood so close, not touching, but he could feel her breath and smell the sweet fragrance of the roses she had pinned in her golden hair; and he imagined he could hear the rapid beating of her heart—or was it his own?

"Thomas," she whispered, her voice sounding as if she were perplexed, unsure of how she was feeling with him so near.

"Katherine," he answered her, and he finally did what he had most wanted to do since he gazed at her across that crowded ballroom. He took her face into his large palms and lowered his lips to hers. He could hear her quick intake of breath, then the soft sigh as she pressed in to kiss him back.

Tenderly, he kissed her mouth, delighting in the poignant connection so evident between them. It was a sense of belonging, a sense of knowing they were meant to be. Thomas felt her tremble, and sensing she must be frightened by the emotions of such an ardent and loving connection, he left her mouth to plant a kiss on her cheek, then her ear before folding her into his arms.

His heart ached that so many problems seemed to plague their relationship, and as they embraced, he sent a silent petition up to God to give Katherine peace and assurance.

After a moment, she stepped away from him, but he moved to take her hand, unwilling to sever their poignant encounter.

"We should not have—" she began in a shaky voice.

"Do not say it, Katherine. You are going to be my wife! It's perfectly acceptable for us to have moments alone together and even share a simple kiss." He gave her hand a gentle squeeze. "I pray you will have no more doubts or fears about us, Katherine. I love you," he stated emphatically, and this time she did not stop him, only stared at him with an indecipherable expression. "Let that be your comfort. Let that be your assurance."

She didn't say anything for a few moments as her gaze lowered to their clasped hands. "I don't think I've ever met a man like you, Thomas. You seem too good to be true—everything that is good and kind." She shook her head as if confused.

"Katherine, do not put me on a pedestal. I have faults like any other man. If Anne were here, I'm sure she'd give you a long list of complaints against me as a husband." He reached out and lifted her chin so she was looking at him. "Will you come to Rosehaven tomorrow? I have decided the manor needs a little sprucing up and want your input since you shall be mistress there," he told her, changing the subject.

She paused as if grappling with her answer. "I will come, though I am not very talented in the art of decoration," she answered finally.

He brought her hand up and caressed her bare knuckles with a soft kiss. "It does not matter. It will be your home, and you should have a say on how it should be styled."

He had a moment of foreboding as one of those fearful expressions crossed her pretty features. But when she nodded, he put it out of his head, intent on enjoying every second with his soon-to-be wife.

ten

"What game are you playing, Katherine!" Theodora snapped as soon as she entered her bedroom.

"What are you doing in my room, Theodora?" she countered, not in the mood to deal with her overbearing cousin.

"Don't be coy with me, Kate! Why have you been lying to me, and why did you give instructions to Ambrose to say you were unavailable?"

Katherine walked to her dressing table and began taking down her hair since it had become loose from the wind. "I don't want to go through with this anymore, Dora. I wonder why I agreed in the first place!" She all but threw the hairpins on her oak dressing table as she spoke.

She heard Theodora sigh and come walking up behind her where her cousin could see her in the large round mirror. "Because you wanted to right a wrong, Kate. A wrong Lord Nicholas Thornton wants to forget," Theodora added quietly.

Katherine's head snapped up, and she stared searchingly at her cousin through the mirror. "What have you heard?"

Theodora turned away with a shrug and with a show of nonchalance picked up a comb from the dressing table, pretending to study it. "It's only servants' talk, you understand. But it's been told to me the earl was heard trying to talk Thomas out of marrying you, that he didn't trust you or something like that." Her eyes slowly rose to Kate's. "He even threatened Thomas. That is why Thomas ran over here in such a hurry to ask you to marry him, dear. He was merely defying his older brother." She put the comb down, bending closer to Katherine's ear. "It makes you wonder if he wanted to propose or was doing it to spite Nicholas Thornton."

Katherine frowned as she looked down at her dressing table, breaking the intense stare. She tried to remember the kiss and the lovely words Thomas poured out to her just moments before, but her bitterness toward Nicholas rose up, making it hard to remember anything but the hurt he'd caused her.

She had been so sure of Thomas's feelings. But now, in light of this news, she had to wonder if he had other motives.

And Nicholas. How dare he try to dissuade his brother against seeing her! He was the one who ruined her good name and made her the subject of ridicule. Why would he not want her to have some sort of happiness in life even if it was with his brother?

The moment she thought that, she felt hypocritical. She wasn't being sincere with Thomas. Did Nicholas suspect she might be using his brother for revenge?

"Oh, what a horrible quandary we find ourselves in, Theodora. God will surely punish us for our deceit!" she cried, throwing her hands over her face.

"Stop the dramatics, Kate. You are beginning to sound like your mother," Theodora said in her practical way. "We must continue to advance our plan." She pulled Kate's hands away from her face. "You must not ignore Thomas any longer. In fact, you must do all you can to reassure him of your feelings—or rather your supposed feelings," she amended.

Katherine thought about that. Not about deceiving Thomas but about how lovely it would be to allow herself to act like his true fiancée—to pretend they would truly be getting married and setting up a household. She could help him with the decorations to his house and get to spend time with him—even if it was only for four weeks.

Katherine felt like a different woman the next day when she met Thomas at his manor. Though Rosehaven was a smaller estate than his brother's Kenswick Hall or any of her family's many properties, the three-hundred-year-old manor had seven bedrooms, a large foyer with an appealing double curved stairway, and a lovely sitting room with a full wall of windows that looked out over the garden. Thomas mentioned this room could be exclusively her own since it adjoined his study and small library.

And for a moment, Katherine let herself dream of painting the room a muted shade of blue so it would appear to be an extension of the sky outside the windows. She could imagine herself sitting on a plush sofa with needlepoint or perhaps reading a book. Thomas would come in often, because he did not want to be without her too long, and when they would have children, there would be blocks and dolls strewn about and perhaps a rocking horse in the corner. . . .

"So what do you think?"

Katherine started as she realized he must have been talking to her and she'd not heard a thing he had said as she studied the room. "I beg your pardon?"

Thomas smiled as he walked over to her and behind her, putting his hands on her shoulders, and began to speak softly into her ear. "I know that look. It is the look all women get when they see a room they'd like to change."

Katherine boldly reached up and put one of her hands over his. "You are right. It is such a lovely room, but—"

"But you can improve it," he finished for her.

She laughed softly. "Perhaps."

He turned her around so she was facing him, and his striking blue eyes studied her. "There is something different about you today. You seem more at ease, happier."

It was so bittersweet to see the relief in his eyes, knowing that in four weeks he would despise her very existence. "I've just decided to enjoy our time together," she told him evasively, not wanting to lie anymore. "And I am quite anxious to help you decorate your lovely manor."

He chuckled as he took her hand and walked her out of the room. "Good, because I have arranged a meeting with merchants for fabrics and furniture and also a seamstress with different patterns for draperies you can choose from!"

All morning long, they talked with the merchants and seamstress, choosing various styles of goods for the manor. Katherine began to realize she actually enjoyed envisioning and suggesting how each room should appear and the major changes that should be made.

Because she'd not been in town, only taking the road between their two estates, she had not heard the reaction of their peers or neighbors. She had not even thought about them since the engagement was announced.

That was why when Sunday came around and Thomas escorted Katherine as well as her sister and cousin to church, she was so surprised by the response they received immediately after stepping out of his carriage.

Not only were the villagers there, wishing them congratulations, but members of the *ton* who were not even part of the church's parish were there, also. The most surprising thing was that the gentlemen, who had snubbed her just weeks before at the ball, were treating her as if nothing had happened.

"What hypocrites," Thomas muttered for her ears only when they had finally broken away and taken a seat in the abbey. "I know I will have to repent for contemplating this, but I would like to take my fist to each one of the rakes who treated you so shamefully before and are now bowing to you like simpering idiots!"

Katherine had to cover her mouth with her gloved hand to

keep from laughing aloud. "Please, don't do that. Then we'd have to deal with another scandal!" she whispered back.

"Who is an idiot?" Lucy asked her in a too-loud whisper that caused the people in the two rows in front of them to turn and look at them. She was sitting on the other side of Thomas and apparently straining to hear what was being said.

"Shh!" Katherine scolded.

And before she could say anything else, Thomas put his arm around Lucy and whispered something in her ear. After that, she sat up in her seat, staring straight ahead.

Katherine shook her head in wonderment. "What did you say?"

"I bribed her," he admitted. "I told her if she was quiet the rest of the service, I'd let her pick a name for my other Arabian."

Knowing her sister's love of horses, she understood how she could be bribed, but what amazed her was that Thomas, who hardly knew her, had been sensitive enough to notice. He had shown the same awareness of her, too. When they were working on his home, he would make sure his cook always made her favorite scones or brewed her coffee instead of tea.

After the service, the ladies were invited back to dine at Rosehaven for a luncheon. Theodora, much to Katherine's surprise, stayed very much subdued, not giving her the usual meaningful glances or hurried whispers. But then she knew her cousin had no reason to say anything because Katherine was playing the part of Thomas's loving fiancée to the hilt.

That was because she so much wanted to be his fiancée in truth. She could admit that. She just didn't know how she could make it happen without Theodora causing trouble.

And Katherine knew her cousin would if she even mentioned she was thinking of changing her mind. How could she not have seen how obsessed Dora was to have revenge on the Thorntons? Her cousin's desire for revenge was not merely to avenge Katherine—she knew that now. But why was this important to Theodora? What would she gain?

She was thankful that, as soon as they arrived at Rosehaven, Mrs. Sanborne was there with Tyler to take her mind off her troubles. Eagerly, she reached for him, but the woman held her off.

"Wait, my lady! You must see his stupendous surprise!" Mrs. Sanborne placed the toddler on the floor, and she watched with pride as he wobbled over to her, then grabbed her skirts before he fell.

"He's walking!" she exclaimed as she bent to pick him up. She turned to Thomas, who did not look surprised at all. "When did he start walking?"

"He has been trying to walk all week, but last night he finally was able to walk from Mrs. Sanborne over to me without falling. We wanted to surprise you," he informed her, his eyes glowing with pride. "I was beginning to worry since he is over a year and still only crawling, but I guess he wanted to take his time."

"Of course he did!" she exclaimed, kissing him on the cheek. "You just wanted to do things your way!"

He jabbered some unintelligible syllables in response, making them all laugh.

After lunch, she, Theodora, and Lucy walked down to the stables. Her sister had informed her she had to "talk" to the horse to be able to name her.

Katherine decided to take Ty with them in his pram. When they arrived, she was about to enter the stables with Lucy, but Theodora stopped her. "Lucy, why don't you go on in, and we'll follow in a moment?" The younger girl merely shrugged her shoulders and skipped away from them.

Katherine had hoped to avoid any conversation since she'd

succeeded in doing so for the last couple of days. Being with Thomas all day certainly gave her an excuse to do that.

"What is it, Dora?" she asked, trying not to seem put out.

"I just wanted to say you are proceeding excellently!" Her eyes glowed. "He doesn't suspect a thing!"

"If you say so, Dora. I really don't think we should be discussing this here, however." She glanced about them to emphasize her point. "Servants do talk, you know."

"I know, I know," she muttered irritably. "I wanted to tell you I have—well—you might say I've added another ingredient to the pot."

Katherine's heart started beating rapidly. "What have you done?" she asked faintly, almost afraid to hear the answer.

"I've written Cameron," she informed her with an evil grin. "And when he gets the letter, I suspect we shall see him before his four weeks are up."

Katherine shook her head in horror. "Do you have no thought for what might happen to either of them, especially Cameron? If he challenges Thomas to a duel, he might be killed!"

Theodora dismissed her words with a defiant lift of her pointed chin. "You worry about things that might never happen, Kate. Stop being so dramatic!"

Kate knew her mother would be furious when she found out, and the sad thing was that it would probably be blamed on her, not Theodora. There was only one thing to do. She was going to have to find a way to tell Thomas and convince him to try any nonviolent things he could to dissuade Cameron from challenging him.

Time is on my side, she thought with some relief. He would not be able to leave school unless he arranged to take his exams early, and that would only cut one week from his four. She'd need that time to think of what to do.

"Theodora, I beg you—do not take it upon yourself to do anything else!" she implored. "Do not forget we are in this together."

"You don't forget this is all a charade, Kate," she spat back. "Those adoring eyes you keep sending him better be make-believe!"

At that point, Ty began to fuss and started trying to climb out of the pram. She grabbed hold of his restlessness as an excuse to get away from her cousin. "Are you wanting to see the horse, little Ty? Let's go see the horsy!" she told him in a singsong voice as she pushed the carriage into the stables and away from Theodora.

She was relieved to find her cousin had gone when they finally came back out. After they rounded the corner to the front of the manor, however, she saw one of the groomsmen leading a carriage and four horses toward her.

She started to ask the servant whose carriage it was, but once she saw the crest on the side of the black shiny vehicle, she knew.

It was the Earl of Kenswick's crest.

Nicholas Thornton must be inside with Thomas!

Panic seized her, but peering down at Ty, she knew she must go back in, that she couldn't stay out in the sun much longer.

"Hey, whose black, shiny coach is that, do you think?" Lucy asked, always the curious one.

"It is Lord Nicholas Thornton's coach."

She looked down at her sister and watched her eyes register with recognition. "Wasn't he the first man you were supposed to marry?" she asked bluntly.

Katherine bit her bottom lip as she unconsciously gripped the pram's handle tightly. "We really must work on your tact, Sister dear," she murmured, her eyes trained on the front door she had to enter.

Lucy made an unladylike snorting noise. "I think you have larger problems than my manners, *Sister dear,*" she retorted.

"Please, Lucy. I'm scared to go in. I don't want to face him," she admitted, her voice growing hoarse with tears.

Then her sister, who was usually a thorn in her flesh, surprised her by reaching over and putting her hand over Katherine's clenched one. "You have Thomas now. Think of how lovely it is you have such a wonderful man you'll marry soon, then perhaps Lord Nicholas will not matter anymore," she said matter-of-factly in a voice beyond her twelve years.

Katherine smiled down at her sister with amazement. "You really are quite smart, you know that?"

She took the compliment as if it were her due. "I know." She then pointed to the pram. "Do you want me to take the pram, or do you want something to hide behind?"

"Maybe too smart," she muttered, throwing her sister a frown. "I'll take the pram, thank you." She proceeded determinedly to the door.

McInnes showed her to the parlor, where they were gathered, and once they noticed her standing in the doorway, all talking came to a stop. Uneasiness filled the room as Nicholas and his wife stood. Thomas stood, too, and came immediately to her side.

"I didn't know they were coming," he whispered in apology as he put a hand at her back and ushered her farther into the room.

Katherine forced herself to look at Nicholas, then his wife. She was surprised to find the bitterness she thought would arise did not consume her as she'd expected. Perhaps it had been her little sister's words that had done the trick; she did not know. But, as she turned from Nicholas's strained expression to his wife, who was smiling uncertainly at her, she felt strangely calm and—

Free.

"You know Nicholas, of course, but I don't believe you have met his wife, Christina," Thomas said quickly as if he were in a hurry to break the awkward silence.

Katherine curtsied, and Christina did the same. "It is nice to meet you, Lady Thornton. Thomas speaks very highly of you," Katherine said first.

The uncertainty left Christina's pretty features as she smiled at her. "Please call me Christina, and I am very honored to make your acquaintance, also!"

Christina, Katherine could tell immediately, was so different from any of the women she knew from the *ton* with her open smile and readable face, but she also finally understood why Nicholas had chosen her. Her uniqueness had apparently been what he had needed to shake him from self-destruction. Something Katherine had been unable to accomplish once he returned from the war.

Nicholas, however, did not share his friendly wife's openness of expression or eager acceptance. He even put a hand on Christina's arm when she stepped closer to Katherine to speak to her as if to protect his wife from her!

Offended by his action, Katherine stayed only a short time more before making her excuses to leave. Thomas stood ready to escort her out when Nicholas stepped forward.

"I would like to walk Katherine out, if you have no objections," he said to Thomas, but his eyes remained watchful and, to Katherine's dread, mistrustful as he trained them solidly on her.

eleven

The moment Nicholas had passed through the door with Katherine and her sister, he asked Lucy if she would give them a moment so he might talk to Katherine alone.

Lucy grudgingly agreed, and suddenly they were alone for the first time since the night he'd broken their engagement. "I won't mince words, Katherine. I need to ask you why out of all the men in England have you chosen my brother to become engaged to?"

She stared at him, aghast at his nerve. "You of all people should know I did not have 'all the men in England' to choose from, thanks to you!" she snapped back.

"So you are using him because you have no other recourse?" he persisted.

Katherine had to take a few breaths to calm the anger that was boiling inside her at his nerve. "How dare you?" she said slowly and distinctly so he could understand every word. "You have no right to question anything I do. I have been through untold anguish, not because of a broken heart"—she wanted to make that clear—"but because the backlash of your actions has ruined my good name. You should be apologizing to me as you told my father you wanted to do, instead of accusing me of using your brother."

They stared at one another for what seemed like centuries before she finally saw a shift in his expression. "I apologize, Katherine," he offered, astonishing her. "I did not mean to come down on you so hard. I—" He stopped and seemed to be thinking of the right words to say. Something that was uncharacteristic of the old Nicholas. "I just don't want to see my brother hurt. He's been through so much, and I suppose I simply want to protect him."

"I'm not going to hurt Thomas, Nicholas. I love him." As soon as she spoke the words, she realized they were true. She did love Thomas Thornton, and she wanted to marry him.

Nicholas, never one to miss much, narrowed his eyes at her. "You seemed surprised by that admission."

She blinked in wonder and looked up at her former fiancé. "I suppose I am," she admitted. "I mean, I knew I was fond of him, but—I truly do love him."

"You haven't told him?" Nicholas was back to sounding protective again. "Whatever were you marrying him for if you did not love him?" he demanded.

Katherine was not intimidated. She folded her arms about her waist and stared him squarely in his blue eyes. "We didn't love each other when you proposed to me," she reminded him.

Nicholas had the good graces to look away in discomfiture, but then he brought his eagle gaze back to her. "I still do not have a good feeling about this match—I won't deny it." He sighed. "But I will say no more about it."

She let out a breath. "Thank you."

"Unless you give me cause, of course," he added, making her want to slap him.

"Kate!" Lucy called to her as she came running to where they were standing on the steps. "Theodora wanted me to let you know the carriage is ready."

"Nicholas, I must bid you good day, but before I go, you need to know, although I hated you for what you did at the time, I can now say thank you. If you had not stopped our getting married, then I would not have met the right man for me."

"Nor I the right woman," he said in agreement. He surprised her by taking her hand and bowing over it. "I wish you happiness, Katherine. And if it is found with my brother, then I cannot begrudge it."

She gave him a tired smile. "Be well, Nicholas," she said quickly as she bobbed a curtsy, then turned to leave.

Excitement churned in her chest as she walked briskly to the carriage. She was in love! For the first time in her life, she loved a man who truly loved her back.

She had so much to think about—so much to contemplate and plan for. But one thing was certain. Under no circumstances could she tell Theodora about her change of heart. On her wedding day, she'd just have to be surprised when she walked down the aisle and took her place by Thomas.

Where she belonged.

☙

"Ye look tae be a bit out o' sorts, my laird," McInnes observed from his post by the doorway, watching Thomas pace back and forth in the foyer.

"He's more than out of sorts, Mr. McInnes," Christina spoke up as she came down the stairs. "He's in love."

"Ah!" The big, middle-aged man nodded sagely as if that answered all his questions. "And tae a verra fine lassie, if ye don' mind me saying so."

Thomas heard both of their comments, but his mind was on what was going on outside the manor. "What do you think they are talking about?" He stopped to run a hand through his thick brown hair, causing it to stand on end.

"Thomas, would you please relax? He is only trying to bring some sort of conclusion to what transpired between them a few years ago," Christina explained reasonably. "Nicholas has felt great guilt over what he did, and I know he only wants to apologize."

Thomas shook his head. "I don't know, Christina. He does not want this engagement between Katherine and me. I do not want him to say anything that will cause her to have second thoughts."

Christina walked up to him and laid her hand on his arm. "Thomas, surely her feelings are not so fragile. She has chosen to marry you, so she must love you. Nothing Nicholas could say will change that."

Thomas's worry only increased as he listened to her. Katherine had not told him she loved him. He did not have that particular reassurance.

All three of them heard the handle of the door being pushed, and McInnes was quick to grab hold of his end and open the door, causing Nicholas nearly to stumble. After he'd regained his balance, he shot a sharp glare at the Scot. "Does he always hide by the door to scare any who might want to open the door themselves?" he growled, directing his question to Thomas.

" 'Tis my job, my laird, tae to be ready and waetin'." McInnes stared back, not cowed by the earl in the least.

"You obviously do not understand the proper conduct of one in your position! If you were in my employ—"

"You would fire him, then rehire him in the next breath as you've done your butler and valet a thousand times," Christina interrupted her husband's tirade in a matter-of-fact tone.

Thomas wasn't sure, but he thought he heard McInnes make a comment about "the overbearing English" before he excused himself from their company.

"Nick," Thomas called out loudly to interrupt the whispered argument his brother and sister-in-law seemed to be having. "I would like to know what was said between you and my fiancée."

Nicholas gave his wife a warning look that seemed to promise they would resume the argument later, but Christina only smiled at him in her charming way. "Before I answer that, I would like to know why you would marry a woman who has not even declared her love for you. Did you not tell me your second marriage would be for love?" Nicholas charged, his frown deepening with every word.

Thomas froze, astounded he even knew. "Katherine told you she didn't love me?" he asked, horrified at the possibility.

Nicholas shook his head in disgust. "No, little brother, she told me she did love you but that she hadn't told you." He snorted. "I told her it was not very—"

"Stop!" Thomas shouted, pushing out his hand toward his brother. "*Katherine*—told *you*—that she loved *me?*"

"Yes, and I told her—"

"She told you—but she didn't tell me," he stated slowly as he tried to understand the reasoning behind his fiancée's withholding this from him.

"Yes, yes, and I—"

"Nicholas, will you stop for a moment?" Christina scolded her husband, grabbing him by the arm and giving it a small shake to get his attention. "Can't you see he is in shock at what you've told him?"

Thomas rubbed his forehead. "What does it mean, Christina, when a woman loves you but does not share it with you?" He pointed to his brother. "Instead she tells her former beau about it!"

Christina left Nicholas's side and came to take her brother-in-law's hand. "Dear Thomas, it simply means she is afraid to expose her feelings to you. As you grow closer and come to trust one another, she will tell you."

"I have to wonder if she is playing at some sort of game," Nicholas stated baldly.

"Nicholas!" Christina gasped. "Consider your words!"

"What are you implying?" Thomas responded at the same time.

Nicholas held out his hands in supplication, his expression

apologetic. "I did not mean to sound so accusing, but I cannot keep my concerns silent. Not when your happiness is at stake, Thom."

Thomas's anger dissipated at seeing the concern in his brother's eyes. "Nicholas, you act as if I am some schoolboy who cannot think for himself." He kept his voice gentle. "I love Katherine Montbatten, and now that I know she loves me, there is no reason to worry."

A self-deprecating smile curved Nicholas's lips. "Then forgive me for prying," he said, but he snapped his fingers as though he'd suddenly thought of something. "Just one thing. I heard Katherine's sister say Theodora was waiting for her. Who is Theodora?"

"She is Katherine's spinster cousin. Vine, I believe her family name is." Thomas became curious. "Why? Do you know her?"

Nicholas shook his head. "I don't think so. I do remember, though, that Father was seeing a local woman years ago after Mother died. I believe her name was Theodora."

"Well, I daresay, there must be quite a few ladies with that name. And, besides, this one doesn't seem the type that would have attracted someone like our father. Keeps to herself, this one does," Thomas commented.

"Mmm." Nicholas looked thoughtful, and Thomas wondered if there were more.

◆

"My dear, you must see the wedding clothes I had made for you!" Her mother held up one garment after another in Katherine's room. Her parents had arrived from London while they had all been at Thomas's manor. "And this"—she paused and held up a beautiful satin gown with pearl accents on the collar, the high waist, and the sleeves—"is your wedding gown. Isn't it stunning?"

Katherine took the gown from her mother's arm with wonder and admiration. "It is a gown made for a princess," she commented in an awed whisper, her fingers reverently brushing over the lovely pearls.

"It is a gown made for a duke's daughter," her mother haughtily corrected. Her attention was caught by Theodora sitting quietly by the bed. "And don't sulk, dear. I did get one for you, too." She pointed to a deep golden gown with ecru-colored lace over the bodice.

Theodora stood up and walked over to the gown. "Thank you, your grace. It's quite stunning," she said, a rare smile on her face.

"Well, of course it is, dear. You are Raven's first cousin and have been an excellent companion to Katherine. It is the least I can do."

As her mother chatted on, Katherine watched Theodora take the gown, then hold it up and glimpse herself in Katherine's oval mirror. Theodora, with her plain gray gowns and her unflattering hair pulled back so severely, had never struck her as someone who would get misty-eyed at a pretty frock.

But then she hadn't truly known her cousin very long. Theodora had come to live with them right after the broken engagement because Katherine's mother thought she needed someone to be with her. Before that, she'd seen her cousin at family gatherings and never paid much attention to her. She did know there was a time when Theodora did not seem so plain—even when she remembered her mother mentioning that Dora was close to becoming engaged, but apparently it hadn't happened.

Had she been jilted as I have? Katherine wondered suddenly. Perhaps that was why she was so determined for her to go through with the plan.

But later, all sympathetic thoughts she may have had for Theodora left Katherine when her cousin began mapping out their plan on the wedding day.

"Now I believe the best thing for you to do is get dressed and pretend you're running late." She glanced down at her notepad and made some sort of mark upon it. "I will tell your family to go on to the abbey, that I'll make sure you get there on time. That is when you will leave and—"

Katherine held up her hand, confused. "Leave? And go where?"

Theodora smiled. "This is where Cameron comes in. When he arrives in a few days, we will tell him of our plan and have him acquire the necessary transportation to get you to the estate in Wales."

She sighed, trying to be patient. "Dora, why do I need to leave?"

Theodora smiled at her as if she were a tolerant schoolmistress trying to teach a slow pupil. "If you stay here, your parents might come back to the castle and make you go through with the marriage. This way you will be gone, leaving a note saying you realized you did not love Thomas and you couldn't go through with the ceremony."

Suddenly, Katherine could not take discussing the plan of revenge anymore. "Dora, I just remembered I need to do something at the abbey," she said hurriedly as she walked to the door.

"What? Should I go with you?" Theodora called after her.

"No!" Katherine cried as she whirled around and held out her hand. "It is something I must do alone," she continued in a slightly calmer voice as she kept backing up.

Theodora tried to argue the point, but Katherine's hands found the handle of the door. She pulled it open and ran quickly out the door, then out of the house.

She didn't understand what or who was compelling her to go to the abbey, but Katherine knew with all her being she had to go there. She had to make things right with God and beg His forgiveness for what she'd planned to do.

It took her only fifteen minutes to walk to the quaint stone abbey and into the cool interior of the empty sanctuary. Tears were already pouring down her face as she ran to the altar and fell down on her knees.

And she prayed. She prayed God would forgive her for the angry thoughts and words she had said about Nicholas and his family. She asked God to bless the love she had for Thomas and make their marriage a strong one, despite the falseness that had been a part of it in the beginning.

Most of all, she thanked God for sending her Thomas and making what she meant for bad turn out so wonderful.

"Lady Katherine, is there anything I can do for you?" She heard the vicar's voice through her sobs and felt his comforting hand upon her shoulders as he knelt beside her.

She lifted up her head, wiping her eyes in the process. "I've been a wicked person, Reverend," she told him, her voice thick and shaky with tears.

The vicar, an elderly man with a shock of curly white hair, nodded sagely. "We all can be a bit wicked now and then. The important thing is you've acknowledged your sin and you've come to the best place to make things right." He patted her on the back. "Did you ask God for forgiveness?"

She nodded with a hiccup. "I want Him to, more than anything."

"That's good, child," he assured her, his eyes crinkling at the corners as he smiled. "Now the only thing you can do is accept His forgiveness and be careful in the future to be a better Christian person."

Katherine felt as though a weight had lifted off her shoulders.

"Oh, I will, Reverend. I shall endeavor to be the very best Christian woman I can be." Then she added, "And the best wife and mother, too."

"Ah! That is correct! I have a wedding to perform in a few weeks. Very fine man you're marrying. Very fine."

Katherine impulsively hugged the vicar, then jumped up from where she'd knelt. She offered a hand to the slim, short preacher and helped him stand, also. "Thank you so much for your comforting words, Reverend. They have helped me tremendously."

When she left the old building, Katherine, for the first time in two years, felt so splendid inside, so full of hope.

The only wrinkle in her happiness was Theodora and her brother, Cameron. But she would not worry about them today. Today she was going to bask in the wonderful feeling that she was finally free from her bitterness and need for revenge.

twelve

Thomas was astounded at the change that had come over Katherine in the last two and a half weeks. She was no longer uncertain in her manner or constantly changing in moods as she had been when they'd first become reacquainted; now she was the loving, caring person he'd always dreamed she'd be.

Katherine, too, had been a tremendous help on the redecoration of his manor, putting her style and special touches in each room of the house. Thomas could not walk into a room without seeing something his lovely fiancée had added or rearranged, and it thrilled him to his very soul to know she was making Rosehaven her home, too.

And then there was Tyler. His son could not have been more attached to Katherine, even if she'd been his real mother. And she treated him like a son, instructing him, dressing him, and even discussing with Thomas about his future education.

Their lives could not be more perfect, except for one little detail.

She had not told him she loved him yet.

He realized they'd not had much time to spend alone, so perhaps the opportunity had not arisen for her to pour out her feelings to him. He knew also that she had shown her love for him in the smiles and the way she freely touched his arm or hand.

Perhaps he wanted too much. After they were married, they'd have plenty of time for talks of love and romance.

Another problem he had encountered the day before was a visit from Katherine's father. The duke had asked him all sorts of questions about whether or not he and Katherine were getting along and if he had anything he needed to tell him before the wedding took place.

Thomas tried to get to the bottom of such an odd interrogation by his future father-in-law, but the duke would not tell him if anyone had talked to him. In fact, Thomas was going to discuss this with Katherine, but all thoughts of the concern left his mind when he saw her.

"We have finally hung the drapes in the library!" Katherine declared, bursting into the room with her sister behind her. "It took us over three hours, and half your staff threatened to quit, but we finally got them up there!"

Thomas chuckled. Both Katherine and her sister were covered with dust. "How did you get so dusty?" He stood up from his desk and walked toward them.

"It is the dust from the old curtains!" Lucy said. "Katherine was trying to direct one of the servants on how to bring the curtain off the rod, when the whole thing fell right on top of my sister." She sneezed then and wearily rubbed her nose. "Unfortunately, I happened to be standing right by her."

"Well, for all your hard undertaking, let me ring for some hot tea and coffee to help calm your—er—dusty nerves." He laughed and pulled a cord beside the grand fireplace in the room.

"Not funny, Thomas. We are truly quite worn out from the ordeal." Katherine started to lower herself onto the red velvet sofa but stopped. "I forgot I cannot sit—your furniture—"

"Is cleanable," he finished for her, placing his hands on her shoulders and gently pushing her down. "You, too," he said to Lucy. He held out his hand to her, but the young girl shook her head.

"If you don't mind, I want to walk down to the barn and see about Rosie," she told them.

Thomas looked at Katherine with puzzlement. "Who is Rosie, Lucy?" He turned back to her when Katherine only shrugged.

Lucy smiled with pride. "Rosie is the name of your other Arabian! Remember that you told me I could name her? I named her after your home, Rosehaven Manor." And before Thomas could say anything else, she skipped out the door that led to a side entrance and was also a shortcut to the stables.

"I am so sorry, Thomas. Of course you should name her something else."

But Thomas shook his head. "No, I promised. But perhaps I can add another name later to make it more fitting, like Desert Rose or something similar."

A knock sounded at the door before Katherine could comment. "A compliment to your staff, Thomas," Katherine told him admiringly. "I've never seen tea delivered so quickly!"

Thomas shrugged, though puzzled. "Perhaps they were anticipating my wanting it. . . ." He walked over and opened the door to the study. It was not the maid, however, who stood there.

McInnes wore the strangest expression Thomas had ever beheld on his butler's face before. It was a warrior's expression, one hard and ready for battle.

"McInnes? Is something wrong?"

" 'Tis an enemy a' yer gate, laird," he whispered menacingly, his jaw muscle flinching with emotion. "If you'd like, I'll taek care o' him fer ye!"

Thomas shook his head in confusion. "What enemy, McInnes? Who are you talking about?" He looked down and realized his butler was wearing a kilt. "McInnes? Why aren't you wearing your uniform?"

" 'Tis the colers o' the clan McInnes, laird. We always wear 'em when trooble is cooming." He leaned forward, and for a second Thomas thought he heard the music of ancient bag-pipes off in the distance. " 'Tis her broother, laird. 'E's coom begging fer a fight."

Then he suddenly understood why McInnes seemed worried.

Apparently Katherine's brother, Cameron, the Marquis of Sherbrooke, was standing at his door and probably none too pleased to hear of the engagement.

"Thomas, what is the matter?" Katherine asked, coming to stand beside him. She, too, gaped at his butler with astonishment.

"Your brother is here."

Katherine's face turned pale, almost white. "Oh, no, Thomas. Please let McInnes send him away. I'm afraid of what he might do," she begged him, clutching his arm.

Thomas patted her hand with reassurance. "Katherine, I cannot hide in fear of him. The sooner I deal with him, the sooner you and I can move on with our lives."

"Show him in, McInnes," he ordered. "Try not to manhandle him too much."

"Aye," the Scot answered with his thick brogue. "I'll get 'im fer ye."

Thomas was a little uneasy at the smile of anticipation on McInnes's face but dismissed it when he looked down at Katherine's troubled features.

"Katherine, please don't worry," he said, trying to soothe her, and led her to a settee. "I'm sure we can discuss our differences like reasonable—"

"Take your hands off my sister, Thornton!" a booming voice commanded from the doorway. Thomas turned in surprise and saw a giant, blond young man bearing down on him with fist closed and ready.

"Cameron, no!" Katherine jumped up and put herself between them.

Cameron paused and took a moment to glare at his sister in disgust. "Get out of the way, Katie, and let me deal with this vermin face to face."

Thomas agreed. "Yes, do sit down, darling." He gently moved her aside, ignoring her protest. "I don't believe I've had the pleasure of meeting you," he told the angry man drolly, determined he was not going to reciprocate his fury.

"Save your niceties," Cameron growled, taking a menacing step closer. "Let's settle this like gentleman, shall we? Pistols. At dawn."

Thomas almost laughed at the absurdity of the challenge. Cameron Montbatten was a young man, probably a couple of years older than Katherine's twenty, and still had much to learn about how a true gentleman conducted himself. But he held on to his bemused mirth and was careful not even to smile, lest he humiliate the brother of his future wife. As it was, he wished he could give the young whelp a good lashing for his impudence.

"Sherbrooke, may I ask just what offense I have committed against you or any member of your family?"

Cameron's clenched jaw jerked with annoyance. "I offered you a challenge, my lord. Will you or will you not accept it?" he demanded, ignoring Thomas's question.

Thomas folded his arms and gave the young man a narrow-eyed stare. "Not until you tell me what I need to know."

"Because your family has caused great harm to my sister's reputation!" he roared, his face a picture of incredulity that he'd have to explain such an obvious reason.

Thomas shook his head and turned from Cameron, walking across the room to motion for the maid, who was standing with uncertainty at the door, to bring in the tray bearing the pots of tea and coffee.

Once she'd set it down and exited the room, Thomas picked

up a cup and saucer. "Would you like tea, Sherbrooke? Or do you prefer coffee as Katherine does?"

Cameron appeared as though he would explode any minute. "Tea? Have you not heard a word I've been saying or"—he stopped, and a sneer spread across his face—"or are you too much of a coward to face me on the field?"

This time Thomas did laugh; he couldn't help it. "Sherbrooke, let me make a few things straight with you," he said, pouring Katherine a cup of coffee. "First of all, I am not the one who hurt or brought shame upon your sister. And, second of all, I am not about to maim or kill my future wife's only brother." He winked at a worried Katherine. "Bad way to begin a marriage, don't you think?"

"How dare you laugh at me!" Cameron charged, shaking a finger at Thomas. "I am sincere in my challenge, and though you did nothing directly, I declare you are just as responsible since you did nothing to stop your brother from doing the deed!"

This time it was Katherine who spoke up. "Cameron, Thomas had just enlisted in the Royal Navy at the time and was preparing for sea." She walked over to him. "Please say no more, Brother. This is none of your concern."

Cameron suddenly turned his rage on Katherine. "What is wrong with you, Kate? Have you no standards at all? Did you not learn your lesson the first time?"

Thomas lost his humor when Cameron grabbed Katherine's arm. He put down the cup and went to take Katherine's other arm. "I've had enough, Sherbrooke. We'd like your blessing, but we don't need it. Your father has given his consent, and that is all we need to get married. Now let go of her arm," he ordered the man, his voice quiet but deadly.

Cameron was young but apparently not stupid. Resentfully, he took his hand away and stepped back. "So you will not meet me at dawn?" he persisted.

Thomas sighed, trying to maintain his patience. "Of course not."

"Then let it be publicly known to you I protest this union and will never accept it!" he stated emphatically.

"Cameron!" Katherine cried. "Please, do not say such things!"

But her brother's expression did not soften as he looked from one to the other, then turned and stalked out of the room.

"I'm so sorry, Thomas," Katherine told him. "He's usually a mild-mannered gentleman. I can't understand why he won't see reason."

Thomas put his arms around her shoulders and kissed the side of her head affectionately. "I am not worried, Katherine. I just do not want you upset about it."

She looked up at him with such feeling that it caused Thomas's chest to constrict with emotion. "I am not going to let anything ruin our wedding day, Thomas. Not even my hotheaded brother."

Thomas smiled, and though he truly wanted to kiss her, he restrained himself, knowing that in two days she'd be his to kiss and hold whenever they desired. He took her hand instead and led her back to the settee. He handed her the coffee he'd poured earlier, then made himself a cup.

They chatted about the changes they'd made to the house, then he remembered the visit her father had paid him.

"Katherine, I had the strangest visit from your father yesterday. Did you know he was here?"

He saw the surprised expression on his fiancée's face. "No, I did not. What was it about?"

Thomas took a sip of his steaming coffee and leaned forward. "He kept asking me if everything was right between you and me and if I had anything to confess to him before we married. Do you know if anyone has said anything to him—anything at all to make him doubt my sincerity to marry you?"

ﻬ

Katherine willed herself not to panic upon hearing of the reason behind her father's visit. Theodora. It had to be Theodora's doing.

She forced a smile, trying to make him think nothing was wrong. "He is just protective of me, Thomas. You know how fathers are," she equivocated.

Thomas nodded, and a sad smile curved his lips. "Yes, I do know. I'm just sad to think my father couldn't be here for the wedding. He always liked you, you know."

Katherine smiled, thankful the subject had been changed. "Why don't you tell me about your father?" she urged him, honestly wanting to know more about the man who sired such a wonderful son.

After that, she didn't stay at Rosehaven much longer.

A half hour later, she and Lucy were in her carriage going home. Her main mission was to find Theodora and confront her with her suspicions. Had Theodora spoken to her father? There could be no other explanation.

thirteen

"Of course I'm the one who has been talking with your father," Theodora admitted without the least compunction when Katherine questioned her. "I tried to talk to your mother also, but we both know she hears only what she wants to and blocks out all the rest."

"Dora, making Papa worried is not going to help—" she tried to reason, but Theodora cut her short.

"I am doing what we had decided *you* would do, Cousin dear!" she charged with a sharpness to her tone Katherine did not like. "Putting doubts in your parents' heads about him will help your explanation when you run away from the wedding! You know this; yet you are doing nothing about it!"

Katherine wearily put her hand to her head, trying to decide what to say and what to do. "Dora, I know we agreed to this, but you must know how busy I've been at Rosehaven."

Theodora made a disbelieving sniffing noise. "That is another one of my concerns, Kate. Either you seem to be playing your part as the loving fiancée so well as to rival any of the actresses on the London stage, or you are beginning to believe the lie. Please, tell me you haven't forgotten our objective!"

Katherine turned from her cousin so she could not see the truth written on her face and walked over to peer out the window. Pushing the lace sheers aside, she muttered, "I don't know what you mean."

She waited for a few long, unbearable moments for her cousin to respond and at the same time dreaded her speaking.

"You have changed your mind, haven't you?" Theodora said

softly, her voice filled with disbelief. "Answer me, Kate! Have you changed your mind?"

Katherine could keep up the charade no longer. Since she'd come to the conclusion she loved Thomas and had made her peace with God, she had gone to great lengths to avoid Theodora; the few times they'd talked, she would say very little. It was time for this whole despicable plan of revenge to come to an end.

She turned slowly and looked the older woman directly in her eyes. "Yes, Dora. I have changed my mind. I'm in love with Thomas and want to marry him."

Theodora began to laugh but not with happiness. It was a crazed sort of laugh that sent chills down Katherine's spine. "You have changed your mind, just like that, eh?" she said in a shrill voice and snapped her fingers for emphasis. "And you thought I would sit back and let you?"

Katherine froze. Was her cousin a little mad? She'd known Theodora had been emphatic and oddly possessed as they planned the revenge upon the Thornton family, but she had not considered her obsession was unnatural.

She wondered again why this mattered so much to Theodora.

Katherine took a breath, then licked her lips nervously. "What do you mean by that, Dora? Are you planning to tell Thomas about our plan? I plan to tell him anyway, so your threats won't work!"

Theodora smirked, her plain face becoming ugly. "I'll do whatever I have to do, Kate. Remember that." She walked closer, and Katherine tried to back up but realized with the window behind her, she had no way to escape her cousin. "I will not let you marry him," she growled no more than an inch from Katherine's face.

"You are scaring me, Dora." She tried to keep her voice

steady and not show the fear churning inside her.

Theodora surprised her by backing up a little and smiling pleasantly. "Don't be a ninny, Kate. I was just teasing you," she explained as if nothing out of the ordinary had just occurred.

But Katherine wasn't fooled by her words or seeming innocence. Theodora Vine was not the teasing sort. All Katherine wanted to do was get away from her, so she pretended to accept her explanation. "Of course you were." She carefully walked around her cousin and opened the door. "I've had a tiring day, Dora—if you don't mind leaving so I can wash up and possibly nap before dinner."

Her cousin smiled at her, but her eyes were hard and cold like ice as she nodded and walked to the door. "Don't worry, Kate. All will be as it should," she said cryptically as she left the room.

Katherine closed the door and leaned against it, her mind racing as to what to do. Part of her wanted to go to Thomas right away and tell him the truth—the plan of revenge, her change of heart—everything.

But another part of her was afraid that if she did tell him, he'd call off the wedding and walk out of her life forever.

Closing her eyes, she prayed, "Please, Lord, guide me in the way I should proceed. I do not want to lose Thomas, not after You have helped me overcome my bitterness and unforgiveness. Help me know what to do—"

A knock sounded at her door, startling her, for she thought it might be Theodora again. "Yes?" she called.

"It's me," Lucy answered from the other side.

Katherine sighed, not wanting to deal with her sister at that moment. "Lucy, I was about to take a nap. Can you come back later?"

"Not unless you want me to tell Mama about the plan," she said in a loud whisper.

Her eyes wide with shock, Katherine threw open the door and dragged her sister inside. "What do you know about that?" she charged.

Lucy shrugged off Katherine's hold on her arm and walked to the bed, plopping down upon it. "I was listening at the door," she explained as if it were the most obvious answer in the world.

"You little scamp!" Katherine roared. "Can I not have any privacy?"

"Not until you move out," Lucy answered. "*If* you move out, that is," she added, her voice mysteriously low.

Katherine shook her head, wondering what her sister would do with the information she had. "Lucy, if you overheard, then you must have heard me tell Dora I will not go through with our plan of revenge. I truly want to marry Thomas."

"It was a stupid plan to begin with," she said critically. "I can't believe you conspired to do anything with Theodora anyway. Can't you tell she doesn't like you?"

Katherine had begun to realize this but was surprised to hear Lucy state it with such conviction. "How do you know this?"

"She resents coming to live here with our family and being the equivalent of a servant." Lucy paused. Katherine waited for her to explain how she would know this. "I heard her tell that to Aunt Constance when she visited last Christmas. Of course our aunt chastised her for speaking so forthrightly, but I heard it all the same."

Katherine sat on the bed next to her sister, her mind trying to think back on all the times she and Theodora had spent together. On hindsight, she could recall times when Theodora's behavior could be interpreted as resentful. "I guess I never realized—"

"You were too busy feeling sorry for yourself," Lucy supplied.

"Are you here to make me feel guilty?" Katherine frowned at Lucy.

The younger girl shook her head. "I'm here to make sure you marry Thomas and not jilt him at the altar."

"Of course I am marrying Thomas. I love him."

Lucy smiled brightly and jumped off the bed. "That is all I wanted to know because I thought it would be quite fun to come and stay with you at Rosehaven in the summer and on holidays!"

Katherine stared at her sister in bemusement. "Behave yourself and keep your mouth shut or you will never get to come!" she threatened with a reprimanding expression.

Her sister, apparently not bothered by the stern warning in the least, merely grinned at Katherine and skipped out of the room.

"Brat," Katherine muttered, thinking her sister was out of earshot.

"I heard that!" came her sister's reply as she poked her head back inside the room with a pouty pucker on her lips.

"Good!" Katherine said before closing the door firmly in Lucy's face.

※

After the meeting with Katherine's father and the confrontation with her brother, Thomas knew he needed to get away from Rosehaven and go to Malbury, where the Kenswick estate was located, to talk with his brother. It wasn't that he doubted Katherine's feelings for him again. On the contrary, when she'd left his home earlier, he felt the affection she had for him, although she did seem concerned about her father's visit.

No, it was that the whole engagement and even before had been riddled with misgivings and reservations—things that shouldn't normally be part of a relationship.

Every day he prayed he could be the father Tyler needed

and the husband Katherine desired and most of all that the little worries and uncertainties would not plague their union as they did now. He knew God had put Katherine in his life. Only God could know what kind of woman both he and Ty needed.

It was just that. . . Thomas dropped his head into his hands and groaned, so very weary of trying to reason it all out.

Finally he could feel the carriage slowing, so he peered out of the small window to determine where they were. It was now dark, but because of the full moon, he could see the majestic site of Kenswick Hall, high upon the hill. He'd spent the majority of his childhood in the old hall, and it never ceased to bring him comfort whenever he would visit.

Because of the late hour, Pierce, the family butler who had been there since Thomas was in his teens, seemed quite put out at having to get out of bed to answer the door. Thomas could tell his clothes had been hastily thrown on, for his shirt was buttoned all wrong and half his thinning hair was standing on end.

"Pierce!" he greeted him. "Sorry to wake you, old man, but I had this need to come to Kenswick, and it just happened to be at a late hour."

Pierce was in no mood, obviously, to act as though he were thrilled. "Could the 'need' not have waited until morning, my lord?" he asked grimly.

Thomas laughed, feeling better already. "Is my brother in bed yet?"

Pierce shook his head. "No, my lord. I noticed they were still in the library on my way to answer the door."

Thomas shook his head with mock disapproval. "It wouldn't hurt him to answer his own door once in a while."

"Beg your pardon, my lord," he returned stiffly. "He is the Earl of Kenswick! He will not open his own doors—not on my watch."

Thomas laughed. "Go back to bed, Pierce. I'll see myself in." He stepped over the threshold onto the marble floor of the foyer.

He glanced back and noticed Pierce still held the door open and was looking out into the night.

"What are you waiting for, Pierce?"

Pierce turned his way. "I was thinking perhaps you brought Master Tyler with you, my lord."

Thomas shook his head with regret. "I'm sorry, Pierce, but I left him at home with Mrs. Sanborne. It was to be such a quick trip that I didn't want to unsettle him by the hour-long carriage ride."

Pierce had such a disappointed look on his long, thin face that Thomas wished he'd brought his son. Nicholas had told him stories about how the butler, as well as many of the staff, had all pitched in to care for the infant when he had first been brought to Kenswick Hall.

"Cheer up, Pierce. In two days' time, Nicholas and Christina will bring Ty back with them from my wedding, since they'll be watching him while I'm on my wedding trip."

This cheered the older man up immensely. Thomas was still smiling about it when he walked into the library and found his brother at his desk reading something. Christina was in the room also, holding some sort of bird.

"Thomas! What a surprise!" Christina greeted him, though she remained seated. "What brings you to Kenswick?"

Thomas's eyes remained on the object squirming around in her arms. "Is that a chicken?" he asked, unbelieving.

"Don't look so shocked, Thom," his brother commented drolly before Christina could answer. "Last week it was a rabbit and the week before a goat that ate half the drapes in the dining room."

"Oh, it did not!" Christina cried defensively. "It only nibbled on the fringe."

"I stand corrected!" Nicholas said with a grin as he stood up and walked to his brother. "Welcome to the Kenswick Animal Menagerie!" He threw his hands wide. "You never said why you are here. Don't you have a wedding to get ready for?"

Thomas hugged his brother and tried to kiss Christina on the cheek, but when the chicken tried to peck him, he blew her a kiss, instead.

"To tell you the truth, I came because I am a little weary, I suppose." He and Nicholas sat down in chairs across from one another, and he went on to explain the confrontations with Katherine's father and brother.

Nicholas seemed thoughtful for a moment, as if he were weighing his words. "Please don't take this the wrong way, Thom, but I have felt unsettled by this whole engagement, as you well know. It just seems odd Katherine would show interest in you when I'd heard she hated me and the entire Thornton family for what she'd suffered."

"Nicholas," Christina said, throwing him a warning look.

Thomas, however, held up his hand to her. "It is all right, Christina. I understand what he is trying to say." He turned back to his brother. "When I first encountered her again at the Beckinghams' ball, I, too, thought it odd she seemed so drawn to me. But you have to realize, Nicholas, there was such a strong connection between us. Perhaps she felt it as intensely as I."

Nicholas nodded. "Perhaps you are right. I pray you are right, for I truly want your life to be a happy one."

Thomas smiled at his brother warmly. "I know you do." He slapped his hands down on his legs. "I've been meaning to ask you, since we are speaking of my life, have you removed the monument yet in the family cemetery bearing my name and announcement of death?"

Nicholas shifted in his chair and looked away. "Uh, not yet, I—"

"He hates to think of destroying it, Thomas, because he worked hours on designing the monument and the statue that bears your likeness upon it," Christina supplied helpfully.

Thomas was astounded by that news. "I did not know you were the one who sculpted it! I had assumed you commissioned it."

"Well, I—"

Christina sighed, interrupting her husband once again as she got up and walked over to the mantel above the fireplace. "He usually carves figurines. He created all of these."

Thomas joined her in admiring the stunningly accurate statuettes of various animals. Each was made with careful detail.

"Is there anything else I should know about you?" he asked teasingly as he studied one particular figurine of a tiger.

"I am sure if you remain at Kenswick long enough, Christina will divulge about everything you ever wanted to know," Nicholas said with mock annoyance.

Christina made a huffing sound of protest. "You make it sound as if I talk too much!"

When Thomas exchanged a knowing look with Nicholas, the brothers suddenly found themselves pummeled with throw pillows.

The next morning, after a restful sleep, Thomas decided to walk through the small, quaint village of Malbury before he rode back to Rosehaven. He thought he would speak with the vicar, who also happened to be Christina's father, and walked the short distance to the cottage that sat adjacent to the church.

Reverend Wakelin seemed to be the same as when Thomas was only a boy. He was now gray and his face lined with wrinkles, but he still exuded energy and a charisma that made him seem younger than his years.

"Lord Thomas!" he greeted before the vicar's housekeeper

could even announce he was there. He was coming from his study and rubbing his eyes, making Thomas think he'd been studying. Christina had told him her father would sometimes forget even to eat when he began digging for information for one of his sermons.

"Reverend Wakelin, sir, it is good to see you," Thomas returned his greeting while shaking his hand. "Did I come at a bad time?"

The vicar waved off his concern. "Of course not. In fact, I needed to take a break, so your visit is more than welcome." He motioned toward a side door. "Come! Let's go into the parlor."

Thomas smiled as he followed. "Is it the one with the lovely paintings your wife painted?"

"The very same," he answered, swinging the door open. There on all four walls hung some of the loveliest paintings Thomas had ever beheld. He'd remembered seeing them as a child but could appreciate the talent behind them more now that he was older.

"They are quite amazing, sir," Thomas commented reverently as he studied one in particular. It was a self-portrait of Mrs. Wakelin holding the baby Christina.

"Please sit and tell me of your upcoming wedding!"

Thomas sat on the sofa and leaned toward the vicar with arms propped on his knees. He told him of the frustrations he'd experienced during his engagement, not mentioning the confrontation he'd had with Cameron. He thought that was better left silent.

"Let me ask you what I asked your brother when he came to me for Christina's hand in marriage." He adjusted his wire-framed spectacles and leaned back in his chair. "Do you love her?"

A smile lit Thomas's face as he thought of his beautiful Katherine. "With all my heart," he answered.

The vicar shook his finger at him. "Then that is all that matters. There is something that happens when two people vow before God to love and cherish one another, especially if they have a relationship with God and mean it with all their hearts. It bonds them together, and when there is trouble, whether it be family or outsiders, those vows will ring out in your heart reminding you that with God you can make it."

Thomas could not wait until those vows were indeed spoken and Katherine was truly his. "I understand what you are saying, Reverend. I do trust in God—I suppose I learned to when I was hanging onto a piece of wood, praying I wouldn't drown in the ocean!" They shared a chuckle, and Thomas stood. "I just need to pray Katherine does not want to bring her companion and cousin, Theodora, to live with us!"

A strange expression passed over the vicar's face as he stood with him. "Theodora, did you say?" When Thomas nodded curiously, he continued. "What is her surname—do you know?"

"It is Vine."

"Vine. . .Vine. . . ," the vicar muttered, scratching his head as if to jog his memory. Then his eyes widened. "Theodora Vine! You have a connection with her, I believe."

Thomas did not think he heard the vicar right. "I beg your pardon, sir? I?"

The vicar nodded. "Well, actually, it was with your father. I believe your father had called on the woman, a spinster, I believe, for a few weeks. It was two or three years after your mother passed away."

Thomas searched his memory. "You know—I believe Nicholas had told me something similar, but we did not think it could be the same woman! What happened to the relationship?"

"Hmm." The vicar hesitated. "I know she was younger than he, but that is not uncommon. I believe he told me she seemed a bit unstable." He nodded vigorously. "Yes, that was it. She was the type of woman who constantly demanded his attention, and when he stopped seeing her, she tried to sneak into his London town home with a knife. Your father, of course, did not press charges, but she was strongly urged by the local authorities to keep away from the earl or else they would go public with the incident."

Thomas frowned. "I wonder why he never told us about the knife episode."

"You were away in school and involved in your own lives. He didn't want you to worry about him, I suppose."

Leaning forward, Thomas told him, "Reverend, this woman has been Katherine's companion, and I've had the feeling she was pushing Katherine to do something. I don't know what it is, but it can't have been good," he added slowly as he hastened to figure out what to do.

The vicar looked at him, his gray eyes deeply serious. "If I were in your shoes, I would urge Lady Katherine to be careful. Miss Vine is the type of woman who could make life unpleasant for anyone who crosses her."

Thomas thought of the way Theodora seemed to try to control Katherine, and his heart pounded a bit faster. If Katherine decided to go against her cousin, whatever that might be, it could be dangerous for her.

Thomas thanked the vicar and left. All the way back to Rosehaven, he tried to convince himself Katherine would be all right since their wedding was only two days away. After that, Thomas would make sure Theodora never bothered either of them again.

fourteen

For a day and a half, Thomas had tried to see Katherine, but it was to no avail. She was either being fitted into her gown or involved in settling in the many relatives who had arrived at Ravenhurst Castle to attend the wedding. He, too, had guests at Rosehaven, which included North, his brother and sister-in-law, and his aunt Wilhelmina.

It bothered him, however, that he did not get a chance to speak with Katherine about her cousin, and when he shared his concern with North, his friend assured him he was no doubt worrying over nothing. But he wasn't reassured, especially when his brother voiced his own worry about Theodora. And when he awoke the morning of his wedding, it was not with the anticipation he should have, but instead he felt a deep foreboding.

His feelings were evidently transparent, for when he joined his family for breakfast, his aunt Wilhelmina picked up on his strange mood. "You are marrying into one of the most prominent families in England, and yet you seem forlorn this morning," she observed in her usual straightforward manner. "If you are concerned at her present social standing, Thomas, I should not worry. Your marrying her has elevated her reputation considerably."

It was Nicholas who responded to that comment. "Aunt Willie," he emphasized, knowing she hated being called that nickname. "None of us is concerned about social standings where marriage is concerned," he stated firmly.

His aunt sniffed. "I daresay you aren't, as you readily proved from your match!"

A stunned silence fell around the table, most everyone aghast that she would be so bold in her criticism. But it was not surprising she felt that way. Thomas knew when his brother had announced he would marry Christina, a common vicar's daughter, Aunt Wilhelmina had tried to tear them apart.

"You go too far, madam!" Nicholas glared at her across the table. He started to leave when his wife grabbed his arm.

"Oh, do sit down, Nicholas. Her words do not bother me in the least," she told him, looking from her husband to his aunt. "Lady Wilhelmina, if you cannot curb your comments and speak of more pleasant things when you are in our presence"— Wilhelmina gasped, but Christina kept talking—"then we shall not let you visit us when our son or daughter is born."

"That is marvelous!" North spoke up with a grin. "Congratulations to you both!"

"You're having a baby?" the older woman asked faintly, clutching her hand at her chest. "This means he will be heir to your title."

Thomas shook his head, as he surmised what this meant to his society-driven aunt.

"Yes, if it is a boy," Nicholas answered, his voice and demeanor now calmed, thanks to his wife.

"Then we have so much to plan for!" She clapped her bejeweled hands together. "We must have the right nanny and then governess—and, Nicholas, you know you must send him to Eton because—"

"We will deal with that as it comes, Aunt," Nicholas interrupted, then looked at Thomas. "What I am concerned about right now is Thomas. You never did tell us why you seem so upset this morning."

Thomas sighed, pushing his food about on his plate with his fork. "It's just a feeling I have—I don't know. I suppose I'm a little out of sorts since I have not been able to talk to

Katherine in two days. I really would like to warn her about her cousin."

"Thomas, you shall have all the rest of your life to talk to her," Christina reminded him gently. "In a few hours you shall be her husband, and it will be within your power to make sure Theodora stays well away from her."

"You are right, Christina," Thomas said, feeling a little better. "I guess I do not want anything to happen to stop us from getting married."

Nicholas stood and put his hand on his brother's shoulder. "Thom, trust in the love you have for one another. I may not have been completely behind this relationship in the beginning, but I do know she spoke the truth when she told me she loved you. Believe in that, little brother."

Thomas held those words close to him as he, with the help of his valet, dressed in his new black suit, with its gray vest and snow white cravat tied expertly at his neck. Christina pinned a pink rose on his lapel, then they, along with Mrs. Sanborne and his son, left in his brother's grand carriage and traveled to the abbey where the service was to be held.

❧

Katherine stood in front of her mother as they stared at their images inside the oval mirror in Katherine's bedroom. She was in awe at how the stunning satin gown with its empire waist and wide pleated skirt transformed her into the bride she'd always dreamed she'd be. The circlet of pink roses around her head, with the lace veil that streamed behind her, completed the look.

"You are so beautiful, dear." Her mother sniffed and put her arm around her shoulders and gave her a loving squeeze. The other hand was dabbing madly at her moist eyes. "I shan't get through the ceremony without staining my own gown with tears—I just know it!" she declared with typical dramatic flair.

It took great concentration for Katherine not to roll her

eyes in exasperation. "Mama, I am sure your dress will hold up fine," she assured her dryly. "And, besides, the pink color complements your features quite a lot. I daresay there will be many comments made about how young it makes you appear."

Her mother immediately stopped crying and nudged Katherine aside a bit so she could see her own image fully. "Do you think so, dear?" she asked breathlessly, tugging at the neckline, then smoothing the skirt. "Yes, I do believe you are correct, Katherine! It is a very good color for me."

Katherine hid her smile behind the bouquet of flowers she'd taken from her nightstand. "You must remember to tell your dressmaker of this so she might search for more fabric of the same hue," Katherine added, feeling a bit guilty she was teasing her mother, though the woman was oblivious.

Lady Montbatten breathed in quickly in a small gasp, and her eyes grew wide. "I shall do that first thing Monday morning!"

"Here you are!" Lucy cried as she came bounding into the room with her usual burst of energy. She, too, was dressed in pink with her thick blond curls tied back with a large matching ribbon. When she saw Katherine, her eyes stared at the veil and ran down the length of the gown to her sister's satin slippers. "You look so beautiful!" she whispered in admiration.

"Oh! Why, thank you, dear!" her mother answered, making the sisters glance at each other with surprised humor. "I was just going down to write a note to my dressmaker about it." She started out of the room but paused to look at Lucy with a critical eye. "Do something with her hair ribbon, Katherine. It appears a bit disheveled!"

"Do you think she is really that capricious, Kate?" Lucy asked with a grin when their mother was out of earshot.

Katherine shook her head with a chuckle. "I don't know. I once thought she may only act that way because it allows her to get away with things a lady normally wouldn't, but now I'm not so certain. She would have to be the world's greatest actress to carry off such a charade over our whole lifetime."

Lucy walked over to her, and Katherine began straightening her ribbon. "Have you seen Theodora this morning?" she asked her little sister. If anyone knew, it would be Lucy.

But the younger girl shook her head. "I haven't seen her since last night, but I did notice Cameron is here."

Katherine was astonished at that news. "I thought he said he wouldn't come."

"You know Cameron," Lucy said with a grown-up tone to her voice. "He pouts, but he loves you too much to snub you on your own wedding day."

Katherine smiled. "I'd hoped he couldn't stay away." She bent and gave her sister a kiss on the cheek. "There you are. Now go down and make sure Theodora is not about causing trouble, will you? I'll be down in a moment."

"I hope she'll be so upset because you are not going along with her plan that she has decided to go away somewhere and not attend the wedding!" Lucy stated fervently.

"Now, Lucy, behave yourself!" she called after her sister, but because she ran out of the room so fast, Katherine was doubtful she even heard.

Katherine's maid came in and applied the last touches to her blond curls. Ten minutes later she was fully dressed, so she made her way downstairs to let her family know she was ready to leave for the church.

But when she stepped into the library where her parents were supposed to be waiting, she suddenly froze.

No one was there but—Theodora.

An uneasy feeling settled over Katherine as she stepped farther into the library, nervously searching about the room. "Where is everyone?" she asked, keeping her voice as steady as possible.

Theodora's lips curved into the most frightening smile Katherine had ever seen. A chill ran down her spine as she tried to assure herself it was only her imagination Theodora seemed so daunting.

"They have gone to the abbey," she answered coolly. "I told them I would ensure you arrived safely and on time." She let out a small laugh. "But of course you won't."

Katherine felt panic building in her chest, and she took a deep breath to try to calm down. She thought about the servants and decided, if she had to, she would scream for their help. "Dora, I told you I had changed my mind, and I meant it," she said firmly, her eyes trying to gauge the distance between herself and the door.

As if reading her thoughts, Theodora began to circle her, putting herself between the door and Katherine. "Ah, but that is not what we planned, Kate. You know that." Theodora stepped closer to the door. "The Thorntons must pay, and this is the only way to do it," she stated as if it were the most rational explanation in the world. "You see, I was once involved with Nicholas's father."

Katherine stood staring at her cousin with unbelief. "What? I never heard about—"

"Of course you never heard about it!" she snapped. "I was staying in Malbury when we met, so very few people knew. He led me to believe I was special to him, then he threw me over for no reason!"

Katherine raced to try to reason with her. "I understand how he must have hurt you, Dora, but this is not going to change your circumstance. This will not make either one of us happy!"

Theodora sneered at her as she clutched the handle of the door. "It will make me happy to see those high and mighty Thornton men suffer as I have suffered! It will make me happy!" she repeated, almost as if she were trying to convince herself of that fact.

Her cousin appeared to be quite mad, completely beyond reasoning. But Katherine was desperate to try. "Please, Dora. When Thomas and I are married, I will help you make another match! We'll arrange parties, get you a new wardrobe—"

"Stop it! Just stop it!" Theodora cried, jerkily shaking her finger at Katherine. "It is too late for that! This is the only way!"

Katherine stood there for a second, stunned when Theodora slipped out of the room, slamming the door behind her. When she heard the key jiggling in the lock, Katherine snapped out of her stupor and ran to the door. She pounded on it with all her might. "Theodora! Let me out! Ambrose! Let me out of here!" she yelled, hoping the butler could hear her, knowing Theodora would not listen.

"There is no one to hear you, Kate!" Her muffled voice came through the thick wood of the door. "So scream your little heart out. It will do no good!"

Katherine continued to scream and bang on the door until she had no strength left. With tears streaming down her face, she finally shuffled over to a chair and fell into it, covering her face with her hands. Heavy sobs shook her thin frame as she contemplated what Thomas would think once she did not show up for their wedding.

❦

Thomas scanned the congregation for the twentieth time in ten minutes, then checked his watch again. *Where was she?* Nervous sweat beaded on his forehead.

He wasn't the only one who was wondering about his absent bride. He heard scattered whispers throughout the building and heads turning to check the entrance to the abbey.

Where was Katherine?

Finally he walked over to Lord and Lady Montbatten. "Your grace," he addressed Katherine's mother. "Are you sure Katherine had a way to the abbey?"

Lady Montbatten seemed a little nervous herself. "Yes,

Thomas. Theodora assured me she would see Katherine arrived safely and on time."

Thomas directed his gaze to the back of the abbey to the person he'd noticed the last time he'd looked for Katherine. "Your grace, Theodora is"—he paused, overwhelmed by the same foreboding he'd felt that morning—"Theodora is here."

"What?" Lady Montbatten cried as she turned in her pew and looked toward the back of the church. "Something is not right here!" She jumped from her seat and hastened to where Theodora was.

Thomas followed her, praying his instincts were wrong but knowing they were right.

Katherine had apparently jilted him.

"Theodora!" Lady Montbatten whispered in a hiss. "Where is Katherine?"

Theodora shifted her eyes from Lady Montbatten to Thomas, her face full of innocence. "She sent me on to the church. She told me she would soon follow."

Thomas didn't understand what was going on, but he knew Katherine would not be coming to the abbey, and he knew in his very soul Theodora Vine was part of the cause.

Katherine's mother sighed. "Well, she must have gotten held up for some reason! I'll send Raven to get her and bring her back here," she insisted. "Wait a few more minutes, Thomas. I'm sure we'll have her here as soon as possible."

Thomas didn't say a word. He merely walked back up to the altar, told the crowd the wedding would be delayed a few moments until the bride arrived, then stood beside the vicar—

And prayed he was wrong and she'd come.

fifteen

Katherine cried so much she finally fell into a restless sleep. She'd done all she could think of, yell, bang on the windows and door—

Pray—

Nothing seemed to work. She had felt so helpless, so despairing. How would Thomas ever understand any of this? How could he forgive her part in it from the beginning?

"Katherine!" a loud voice bellowed over her, causing her nearly to fall out of the chair. "What are you doing here?" her father demanded, once she had looked up at him with bleary eyes.

She pushed her tangled veil out of her face and tried to get her bearings. "How did you get in?"

Her father blew out a breath of frustration. "How do you suppose I got in, young lady? I opened the door!"

Katherine shook her head, knowing she must not hear him right. "But it was locked!"

For the first time in her life, her father directed a frown of pure disappointment upon her. "It was not locked."

"But—"

"Do not insult me by lying, Katherine. I've been looking for you for over forty minutes around the property, thinking you might have been kidnapped or crashed in your carriage. But when I realized the carriage had never left the stables, I came inside to search for you." He shook his head. "I never thought you'd do something like this, Katherine. I am ashamed of you."

Tears were once again spilling from her eyes. "Papa, you don't understand. Theodora—"

"Yes, she informed me you sent her ahead to the abbey. She's also been looking about the house for you!" He stared at her as if he didn't know her at all. "Did you do it for revenge? Did you plan this whole thing to bring shame upon the Thornton family?"

Katherine grabbed her father's arm, her eyes pleading with him to listen to her. "No! Papa, you must hear me—"

"Instead," he continued as if he didn't hear her, "you have brought more shame upon this family."

With that, he shook off her hand and walked to the door.

"Papa! I didn't do this deliberately! Papa!" she yelled, but he never turned back as he left the room.

Katherine rubbed her eyes, trying to clear them. Walking out into the hallway, she turned in the direction her father had taken. Abruptly she stopped, realizing that speaking to her father was not her top priority. Instead, she ran in the opposite direction to the front door.

Perhaps if she spoke to Thomas, she could explain. Make him understand what had happened.

She did not know what compelled her to stop by the abbey first, but she asked her coachman to do that very thing.

As she let herself into the church, she was assaulted by the sweet smell of the roses her mother had decorated with. On each pew end was a small bouquet, and in the very center of the altar was a huge one with both pink and white roses intertwined with the same colored ribbons.

Beside the bouquet, sitting on the front pew, she saw him. Thomas was there, bent over slightly; his eyes seemed to be focused straight ahead, staring at—nothing.

Her heart felt as though it were breaking as she slowly walked up to where he sat. The floor creaked beneath her slippers, but he did not turn or make any movement of acknowledgment at her presence.

A few feet from him, she stopped. Taking a deep breath, she called softly, "Thomas."

He stood then and slowly turned toward her, his face swathed with hurt and betrayal. Those blue eyes that had gazed lovingly into hers only a few days before now stared with stark coldness.

"Thomas, listen," she began, her voice shaking. "This was Theodora's doing. I tried to—"

"I can't believe I've been so gullible," he ground out bitterly, making a slashing movement with his hand. "I had a feeling all along you and your evil cousin were up to something. I never dreamed you would go to such elaborate lengths." He ran his hand through his already mussed hair. "Or perhaps I did but did not want to believe it," he added with a self-deprecating murmur.

"It's not like that, Thomas." She realized it was time to tell him the truth. "You see, I did set out to hurt you, but I changed my mind after I met you. It's just that Theodora would not accept it. She locked me in the castle. I couldn't get out!"

"You mean you set out to convince me to marry you, all along knowing you would never go through with it?" he asked, focusing on her first sentence. He appeared confused. Katherine hurried to explain.

"Yes, Thomas, but I changed my mind! Don't you understand? I was hurt and bitter over what happened with your brother and how the *ton* turned against me. Theodora convinced me this was the only way to avenge myself. But I couldn't do it."

An appearance akin to revulsion spread across his face as he stared at her. "That you could even think of hurting an innocent man, a man who was falling in love with you, horrifies me, Katherine. You are not the person I thought I knew."

With one last look, he brushed past her. Katherine turned and ran after him. "Thomas, I've changed! I fell in love with you, too. I even asked God for forgiveness for the sin I had planned to commit! Please, believe me."

He kept walking, and she followed him outside, in the shaded courtyard of the abbey. She expected to see his coach waiting for him, but when she saw only a horse, she thought his family must have taken it back to Rosehaven. He stopped and turned toward her when he reached the animal. "You know, Katherine—I have waited weeks for you to tell me you love me, but you didn't. You can perhaps understand why I'm having trouble believing you now."

"Thomas!" she cried, tears pouring from her eyes as she watched him mount his horse and snap the reins to urge him forward. "But I do love you, Thomas. Believe me. Please, believe me."

Katherine realized her words were falling on deaf ears. As he galloped away, she fell to her knees, her wrinkled wedding gown spread about her as great sobs shook her body.

"My lady!" her coachman called, running to her.

"I've lost him," she muttered incoherently. "I can't believe I've lost him—"

"I'm sure 'tis not as bad as all that, my lady." He managed to lift her to her feet.

Katherine allowed him to lead her to the carriage and tuck her in safely. She lowered her gaze to her gown and saw the dirt stains that now marred the once lovely satin material.

She wished with all her heart God could remove the stain in her heart as easily as her maid could remove the stains from her wedding dress.

❧

"Are you all right, Thom?" Nicholas entered the sitting room where his brother was staring out the window.

"Have you come to say I told you so?" he asked bitterly, wishing everyone would go home.

Thomas heard Nicholas sigh and his footsteps come nearer to him. "I think you know better than that," he answered quietly, making Thomas feel shameful at his malevolent attitude. "The vicar came by a minute ago, but I told him you weren't receiving anyone."

Thomas nodded, his eyes still fixed ahead, staring at nothing. "I appreciate that."

The brothers lapsed into silence, then Thomas saw Nicholas move beside him on the other side of the wide picture window. "He did say, however, that he saw you talking to Katherine outside the church." Nicholas cleared his throat as he cut his gaze over to his brother. "Well, no—that is not exactly what he said. I believe he told me you were yelling, and she was crying, running after you." Nicholas turned to stare fully at his brother. "What happened? Why didn't she come?"

Thomas made himself face his brother. "You were, indeed, right when you said it seemed an odd coincidence she happened to turn her attentions to me. She was conspiring with her cousin, Theodora Vine, to get me to the altar so she could call it all off, thus vindicating the hurt you caused her. In other words, she was using me to hurt you."

Nicholas shook his head, dumbfounded. "You can't be serious! I thought she'd turned to you because you were the only man available to her, not because she had a malicious agenda!"

Thomas closed his eyes briefly and tried to block the sharp pangs of hurt and disappointment that pierced his heart and soul. Instead, he tried to focus on the emotion that was easier to express—his anger. "I cannot believe I have been so foolishly misled," he spat out, talking more to himself than to Nicholas. "I knew something was amiss; yet I kept pursuing her and trying to make it work."

Nicholas gripped his arm. "Thomas, you are not a fool! You simply loved her, and you cannot be faulted for that!"

"I even prayed I could be the right man for her, Nick. In my stupidity, I assumed God had put us together and she would be the perfect mother for Tyler and all our children to come." He swallowed hard, trying to chase away the bitterness that seemed to clog his chest and throat. "She seemed to love Tyler, Nick. How could I have misunderstood?"

"God can work this out, Thomas. What did she say to you? Why, if her plan was to abandon you at the altar, did she show up later? Surely by staying around she would have to bear the chastisement of her father and mother."

Thomas had a picture of Katherine's tear-stained face as she pleaded with him to forgive her. "She said she had tried to make it to the wedding because she had fallen in love with me and had changed her mind about her plan." He let out a snort of disbelief. "She had the audacity to blame her absence on Theodora locking her in a room. Why wouldn't the servants let her out then?" he asked, throwing his hands up in the air.

Nicholas frowned thoughtfully. "But, Thomas, what if it's the truth? Katherine is not an evil person by nature. I could quite believe bitterness made her concoct the plan, but guilt and love for you would not let her go through with it."

Thomas was not ready to hear reason. He turned his heated gaze to his brother. "She purposely tried to get me to fall in love with her, and I"—his voice cracked, and he paused a second before continuing, his voice more solemn—"and I did, Nick. I love her still, and one day soon I will forgive her misdeeds against this family and me. But I will never allow her back into my life again."

Nicholas slammed his hand down on the white, wooden window seat, startling his brother. "Don't do this, Thom," he growled at him. "Remember what bitterness did to me? Dwelling on bitterness and anger separates you from everyone you love, and most important it will separate you from God." He took Thomas's shoulders in his hands and shook him gently. "And living a life without God's love is the coldest, most miserable world you could possibly live in."

Thomas shook off Nicholas's grasp. "First you warn me against her, and now that she's shown herself to be conniving and untrustworthy, you want me to give her another chance. What do you want me to do, Nicholas?" he asked, feeling the desperation of his situation closing in on him.

"You must do whatever you feel God needs you to do," Nicholas answered, his eyes and voice intense. "Push away the hurt and emotions, then do what your heart is urging you to do."

Thomas did not have to look deep within himself to know what he should do. He loved Katherine with all his heart and soul. Nicholas did not realize how tremendously he wanted to believe her, wanted to be assured she truly loved him.

But he could not go to her. Perhaps it was pride or some other strong force that kept hardening his heart toward believing her, but it was there.

"I can't do anything right now, Nick." He finally spoke the only truth he knew at that moment.

Nicholas sighed and put his arm around his brother for a brief hug. "I will pray you do it soon, then."

"Please, give my apologies to your wife and North that I cannot entertain them tonight. I fear I need to be alone," Thomas said once they stepped apart.

Nicholas nodded. "We had all planned to leave in the morning." He walked to the door but turned to give his brother a look of concern. "I will come if you need me. North wanted me to convey the same message to you."

Thomas nodded and watched him leave. After that, he did not know how long he stood and stared out the window, replaying the day over and over in his mind, reliving each and every horrible minute of it.

His thoughts were interrupted when Mrs. Sanborne hesitantly entered the room, asking if he'd like to tuck his son into bed as he did every night.

He almost declined, but suddenly he had an urge to hug his son, to tell him he loved him no matter who did or did not come into their lives.

sixteen

The scene that followed the next day was not a pleasant one. Katherine had finally admitted to her father her and Theodora's plan. She also told him she could not go through with it. She explained that her cousin had locked her in the room, but because the room had been unlocked, he had not believed the last part.

That did not mean he would allow Theodora to get away with what she'd done.

He summoned Theodora into his meeting with Katherine, and she knew the older woman had some idea of what it was about by the speculative gleam in her eyes as she entered the study.

Katherine prayed that whatever excuse her cousin gave, it would not be more convincing than the truth she'd already told her father.

"Theodora," Lord Montbatten began, his tone hard and serious as he looked up at her from his desk chair. "Sit down, please. I have something I need to discuss with you."

The usually collected woman appeared very nervous as her gaze darted from Katherine back to Lord Montbatten. "Your grace, if it is about the wedding, I tried to bring Katherine with me, but she—"

"Theodora!" he thundered, causing her to cease her prattle. "Do as I have asked and sit down!"

With pinched lips, the older woman did as he ordered and sat on the edge of the leather chair across from him.

The Duke of Ravenhurst minced no words. "Because of

your dire situation two years ago, I allowed you to come live with us and be my daughter's companion. And though I knew about all the trouble you had caused the late Earl of Kenswick, I had your promise you would behave in a ladylike manner, helping my daughter through her difficult time."

"Yes, your grace. I fully appreciated your generosity—"

"You do not 'appreciate' anything, Theodora Vine. I believe you actually resent the post you have been given here," he inserted forcibly.

Theodora's face held an innocent expression Katherine knew all too well was faked. "But, your grace, I—"

"Because of this latest scheme you and my daughter have conspired, I can no longer allow you to stay and influence any more members of this family."

All manner of pretense left Theodora's face, and a look of pure hatred masked her features. "How easy it is for you to throw away an unwanted, poor relative. You sit in your many homes and castles and presume to cast judgment on all you deem undesirable." She stood, her fists balled tightly at her sides. "What about your own daughter? She has obviously planted all sorts of lies in your mind against me. Did she also tell you of her own deceit?"

"Theodora, I told him everything," Katherine answered. "I am taking no fault away from myself in the plan. I only wanted him to know I had decided not to go along with it. I told him the truth."

Theodora threw back her head and let out a crazed laugh. "Your truth, Katherine. That does not mean it is the real truth!"

"Enough!" Lord Montbatten roared. "I do not know what is going on here, but I only know I will not tolerate this any longer!"

"I will not allow you to throw me out, sir. I will leave on my own accord. You do not have all power over me, you know!" Theodora declared in a triumphant sneer as she spun around and started out of the room.

"I am afraid I cannot allow you simply to walk out of here when you can easily come back to harm either Katherine or anyone else in the family."

Katherine turned to her father in surprise and saw Theodora also looked very confused. "What do you mean by that?"

"I have arranged for you to leave here with my sister and travel with her to France. She is a widow, as you know, and needs help with her eight children. I told her you would be available."

Theodora was not cowed by his arrangement. "You cannot make me go with her! I will simply refuse! Do not think I am completely without friends or resources. I will go elsewhere."

Lord Montbatten leaned forward as he narrowed his sharp gaze on his cousin. "You either go with her or I shall tell the authorities to renew the charges against you because you have conspired to bring ruin to a member of the *ton.*"

Katherine suspected Theodora knew she had no recourse. The older woman marched out of the room but not before she stopped where Katherine was sitting and smiled at her coldly. "Welcome to the world of spinsterhood, where you are at the mercy of self-serving relatives who care nothing for you except what you can do for—"

"That is quite enough, Theodora!" Lord Montbatten roared.

"Good-bye, Dora. I hope you'll be happy," Katherine told her quietly. For the first time, she truly felt sorry for the woman and prayed she'd allow God to come into her life and help her.

But for now, Theodora only sent her a heated look before sweeping through the door.

When Katherine awoke the next morning, her aunt had left with Theodora.

After that, the matter was dropped, but it was clear she would bear the result of her actions for a long time.

And she did. For in the two weeks that followed, Katherine was sure she had never felt so alone in her entire life. Though she'd once again tried to explain what had happened, neither her father nor her mother spent any time with her. At dinner she was largely ignored, except for Lucy's attempt at bringing her into the conversations. But even then, all would fall silent, then they'd begin a new subject—one she could not be part of.

Katherine knew what their silence was about—though they believed Theodora had kept her from attending the wedding, the whole event would not have happened if the two cousins had not contrived the scheme in the first place.

Lucy was most surprising at her acceptance that Katherine was truly sorry for her deeds. Even Cameron, before he'd left a week earlier, had told her that while he still despised Nicholas Thornton, he was sorry she had been hurt over the ordeal.

He was not, she noted, sorry the Thorntons were embarrassed over the situation.

As she paced back and forth in the foyer of the castle, waiting for a reply to the letter she had sent Thomas, she wondered if this letter, too, would be rejected as all the others had.

Day after day she'd written him, and every time her letter came back with the seal still intact and unread.

Christina, Thomas's sister-in-law, had even written her a letter, urging her to try to see Thomas and mend the relationship. *He's not doing well*, she wrote in her scrawling handwriting. *He won't even allow Nicholas to come out to Rosehaven to see him.*

She went on to tell her own story of how she had to badger Nicholas into opening himself to other people again when he'd returned from the war. Even when he rejected her, she had gone to his house, finding excuses to run into him until he finally gave in to her.

So, just two days ago, Katherine had tried to do as Christina suggested. She went to his house and told McInnes she would sit on the front step until he came out and talked to her.

Apparently the picture of her sitting alone deep into the afternoon and the beginning of night could not induce him to care enough to speak with her. She finally left, her faithful coachman having waited for her all day to take her home.

The large brass ring on the outside of the main door to the castle sounded loudly inside the marbled foyer. Katherine ran to the door as Ambrose opened it and took the letter from the boy who had delivered the note.

She held her breath as Ambrose closed the door and turned to her, handing her own letter back to her. There was pity in the older man's eyes as she slowly took the folded papers bearing her intact seal.

Though tears stung her eyes, she avowed she would not cry in front of her father's servants anymore. She'd done it so much, he'd sent the doctor over to check her "mental health."

She wasn't crazy; she was just so desperate to get in contact with Thomas. Somehow, someway, she had to let him know she would not give up on her love for him.

Deciding she had to get out of the castle for a bit, she ran to get her light shawl from her room and headed out toward town.

She was surprised to see Lucy by the gate that surrounded their property. She was without her governess or a maid, which meant she had sneaked out without her parents' permission.

"Where are you going alone?" Katherine asked in her typical big-sister voice she knew irritated her little sister.

She saw a bit of guilt on Lucy's face as she answered evasively, "I just wanted to be by myself for a while. Perhaps pick flowers near the forest."

Katherine, in a hurry to get away, was in no mood to argue with her sister, so she gave in to her. "Well, do not stay out too long. Mama will worry if she chances to look for you."

A satisfied smile curved Lucy's lips as she skipped off without so much as a thank-you.

Katherine let go a deep sigh as she began the short walk to the village. She noticed the summer flowers blooming in full color around her, and it went to great lengths to restore her spirit.

At moments, during the two weeks, she had felt so alone and wondered if even God had abandoned her. But surrounded by His beautiful plants and trees and the warm sun shining on her face, she knew He had never left her. He was in everything around her, reminding her that when she was down, He'd be there to lift her up.

At last she entered the village, and her reception by the people of the village would probably have been laced with more frostiness had she not been above most of them in station. As it was, they were polite but not talkative, and Katherine could not blame them for their judgment. She had done a very bad thing; even if the end result had not been her fault, she had brought it on herself.

She had gone into the bookstore, which usually never failed to take her mind off her problems; but today it did not. She wandered around for about ten minutes, then decided to stop by the village inn to get a cup of coffee before she started back on her journey.

Katherine had walked only a few feet when unexpectedly a man stepped directly in front of her from out of a shop. She stumbled to gain her balance, and when she looked up to mumble an apology for not seeing him, she froze.

There Thomas stood, staring at her with as much surprise as she was at him.

"Thomas! I can't believe it is you—"

Before she could finish her sentence, he turned away from her, giving her the rudest direct cut she'd ever received from anyone.

Ignoring the pang of hurt that pierced her heart as he walked away, she tossed all protocol to the wind and ran after him, not caring that she was making a spectacle of herself.

"Thomas! Please talk to me!" she called as softly as she could when she finally reached him and grabbed hold of his arm. He stopped when he felt her and after a tense moment turned and stared coldly into her tear-filled eyes. "Why won't you let me explain? Why won't you at least give me a chance to—?"

"I know all I need to, Katherine. Frankly, anything you could tell me right now I would be disinclined to believe." She gasped, and he became grimmer—seemingly more determined. "I'm sorry, but that is how I feel."

"But I told you I had changed my mind!" she cried fiercely, hoping he'd see the love pouring from her gaze—from her expression. "I love—"

"Do not speak of it, Katherine!" he insisted in a stern whisper. "It is over and done with. Now please, cease in your attempts to contact me."

"I won't!" she declared. "I will not give up on us, Thomas. Not until you listen!" Her voice had risen to the point that anyone coming onto the street could hear every word.

He merely shook his head at her, disappointment etched on his handsome face. "Katherine, you need to stop. You are embarrassing yourself and me. Good-bye."

She watched with disbelief and a wounded heart as he turned from her. It was pride that held her back this time. She'd pleaded with everything in her, and he'd rejected it.

She had nothing else to give. No more words to say.

He'd given up.

Perhaps she should, too.

Suddenly, she became aware that everyone who had been in the village shops was now lined on the dirt street, staring at her as if she were mad.

Everything, even her dignity, had now been stripped from her. Gathering as much fortitude as she could, Katherine held her head straightforward as she walked down the street, ignoring the glaring eyes and curious faces.

Once she was out of their sights, she allowed her tears to fall, but she vowed it would be the last time she'd allow herself to cry over Thomas Thornton.

She had only God now. He loved her. He had forgiven her.

It was a good start.

❧

Thomas felt as though his heart were breaking into pieces as he turned from Katherine and walked away.

He'd been so close to forgetting his pain, forgetting his feelings of betrayal, and simply pulling her into his arms. He loved her so much it had been agony turning her letters away each and every day.

But his pride had stood in the way. His manly pride that stopped him from forgiving her as he knew he should.

Deep inside, he knew she wasn't lying to him when she declared her love. But he could not believe no one could have heard her cry out, if Theodora had indeed locked her in the room.

It had been the one sticking point as he'd deliberated over the circumstances of that day. The Montbattens had more servants than anyone he knew. He could understand Theodora's fooling one of them into going along with her plan, but the entire staff?

Not likely.

If only he knew for sure. Could he know?

He entered his manor and stopped when he saw the uncomfortable expression on McInnes's face.

"What is it, McInnes?"

" 'Tis tha' young lass, my laird. I couldna turn tha' puir thing aweey," his butler said hesitantly, motioning toward the sitting room Katherine had liked so much.

Thomas looked at the open doorway but could not see inside the room. Was he talking about Katherine? Surely not, he tried to assure himself. There was no way she could have beaten him to the manor.

"What poor thing—I mean, who are you talking about?" he amended, shaking his head, confused.

"He's talking about me," a familiar voice spoke, and Thomas glanced back over and found not Katherine but her sister, Lucy, standing in the doorway. She was not wearing her normal carefree, happy expression; instead she looked upset, with her arms folded and her toe tapping the floor in annoyance.

"Lucy? What are you doing here?" he asked, walking with her back into the sitting room.

He showed her to one of the plush seats her sister had picked out for the room and sat across from her. Lucy seemed to take an enormously long time in smoothing her skirts and getting settled in the chair. "I have come on a matter of great importance," she announced formally, her expression more adult than child.

Thomas didn't want to upset the girl, but he was in no mood to discuss her sister. "If this is about Katherine, Lucy, it is none of your business—"

"Oh, yes, it is my business!" she declared, interrupting him. "You don't have to listen to her crying all day long and holding those sad little letters you return to her unopened." She took a breath and scowled at him. "Hasn't she suffered sufficiently? Or are you going to let her go on like this indefinitely?"

Thomas tried not to be stirred by Lucy's words, but the vision of Katherine holding those letters and tears streaming down her face made him feel ill.

"It is my intention to go on with my life, Lucy," he told her gently, not believing his own words. "Your sister will, too."

Lucy shook her head sadly at him. "It wasn't her fault Theodora locked her in the room. My cousin had even made sure every servant was out in the garden, setting up for the party." She sniffed. "I can tell you Ambrose was none too happy about that. Said it was quite beneath his dignity."

Every muscle in Thomas's body froze at her words. He didn't take a breath as he contemplated what that meant. "I beg your pardon, but did you say there were no servants in the house? None at all?"

"None!" Lucy assured him. "I know because Theodora bragged about it to Cameron—because, of course, he was glad the wedding didn't take place," she said matter-of-factly. "And when I asked Katherine about it, she said Theodora told her the same thing. My sister yelled and pounded on the door until she grew tired and cried herself to sleep. Theodora came back home with my father, and while he was out looking around the estate, she came in the house and secretly unlocked the door so it would look as if Katherine had deliberately stayed home from the wedding."

Thomas closed his eyes as he thought of what Katherine had gone through, especially when he did not believe her. "Lucy, do your parents know any of this?"

The young girl nodded her head, her bright golden curls springing about with the movement. "Yes, but I am not sure they believed her about the house being empty. I've tried to talk to them, but they won't listen," she said as if she were terribly put out about it. "Father keeps telling me he is too busy to talk, and Mother keeps crying and lamenting how they will never be able to face the *ton* again." She leaned forward and with a serious face confided, "It's quite daunting to live in a household where everyone is so caught up in their own feelings they won't let anyone help them feel better."

Thomas stood up and put out his hand to her, pulling her up with him. "I have to go to Katherine," he said quickly, knowing he could wait not a minute longer.

Lucy's eyes lit up with hope. "You are going to forgive her?"

Thomas put his hand on her smooth jaw with affection. "I will do better than that. I am going to ask *her* to forgive *me.*"

Lucy nodded sagely. "Excellent plan. I think that will do quite nicely."

Thomas smiled at her and gave her a big hug. "Would you like to ride with me back to your home?"

Lucy surprised him by declining. "Oh, no. I snuck out to come and plead Katherine's cause to you. So I will have to sneak back in!"

Thomas laughed and walked hurriedly with her out of the room.

seventeen

Thomas decided to take Sultan since the horse could get him there faster than a carriage or walking. As the wind ripped through his hair and clothes, Thomas prayed it wasn't too late. He knew he'd hurt Katherine today by his coldness and by allowing her to make a fool of herself in front of the entire village.

He was so caught up in his thoughts that he didn't see a low branch hanging over the path. Leaves and dense branches hit him squarely in the face, almost knocking him off his horse.

He slowed Sultan down a bit and gingerly touched his stinging cheek. He checked his hand and saw a smear of blood on his fingertips. Thomas grew aggravated at himself for letting the mishap happen. He needed to present a good picture of himself when he arrived at the castle, and here he was, his hair askew, his clothes riddled with leaves and bark, and his face bloody.

Not exactly respectable standards.

But it really didn't matter, he tried to assure himself as he took out a linen handkerchief from inside his coat pocket and held it against the scrape on his face. Urging Sultan on at a slower speed, he knew the only thing that mattered was making Katherine believe how sorry he was for doubting her.

In hindsight, Thomas wished he'd heeded his brother's advice and tried to remember the time he'd spent with her in the weeks leading up to the wedding. Now he could remember how loving she was with him, how caring she was toward

Tyler, and how beautifully her eyes lit up when they had shared that kiss.

He'd taken great measures not to be so forthright again, but he had wanted to kiss her. He had wanted to take her in his arms, and now he had no doubts she wanted to be near him as much.

Once he arrived, he handed over Sultan to a stable boy with instructions to wait a moment before taking him to the stables in case Katherine would not see him.

A less than friendly Ambrose opened the door and reluctantly showed him in, making him stand in the grand foyer to wait for the duke.

He was taken aback when the duke rushed into the room, spouting apologies even as he came through a doorway. "I am so glad you've come, my lord. I must apologize again for my daughter's behavior. She used to be such a good girl and—"

Thomas held up a silencing hand. "Your grace, please," he interrupted before he became irritated that the man would say anything else about his daughter. "I did not come here for apologies. I came because I must see Katherine!"

The duke frowned and gaped at him in a moment of stunned silence. "What happened to you, son? Were you set upon by highwaymen?" he asked as he took in Thomas's rumpled clothes and scraped face.

"It was a branch," he muttered, agitated at having to answer when he needed to speak to Katherine. "Now about your daughter, your grace, I—"

"Why do you need to see her? Hasn't she tried to apologize to you in letters?"

"Yes, and I thoughtlessly sent them back unanswered," he admitted. "But you have it all wrong, your grace. It is I who needs to apologize to her. I had thought she was lying when she said Theodora had locked her in her room."

The duke shook his head. "Yes, yes, but I still am not sure I believe that. Surely she couldn't have routed all the servants out of the castle! It's been my belief Katherine stayed home, and by the time she realized she wanted to marry you, it was too late. So she lied," he theorized.

"But she didn't," Thomas insisted, hoping he could set the matter straight. "Theodora admitted to Cameron she had done the deed and devised a scheme to get all the servants out of the castle so she could accomplish it. Katherine apparently cried until she finally fell asleep in exhaustion."

"Oh, dear. I feel quite guilty for not believing her. I have been quite severe upon her for the last two weeks," the duke told him, his gray eyes troubled.

"Ambrose told me Katherine had not returned home from her trip to the village. Do you know where she might have gone?" Thomas asked, his voice growing more urgent as the need to see Katherine increased.

He was devastated when the duke shook his head sadly. "I am afraid I don't know. You can wait for her here if you'd like."

"No," Thomas answered emphatically. "I have to find her. I have to let her know I believe her."

"You might find her either in the moat or by the bridge that spans across the narrow part of the lake, my lord," Ambrose answered, stepping into the room.

"The moat? Do you mean my daughter spends time in that great ditch around the castle?" the duke asked, clearly distressed by this. "She would almost have to use her hands to get in or out of there. Quite unladylike! Quite!" he stressed, apparently already forgetting he owed his daughter an apology.

Lucy was right about her parents. They were not the most attentive in the world. "Regardless, your grace, I will go and look for her."

He turned and walked toward the door Ambrose already held open for him. "I pray good news about renewed wedding plans will follow upon your return, my lord," the old butler whispered.

Thomas paused a moment to pat him on the arm with an assured smile. "I'll do my best, Ambrose!"

"Excellent, my lord."

The moat, unfortunately, was empty, so Thomas ran down to the lake, stepping over bushes and foliage, praying he wouldn't trip and further damage himself.

He came upon the clearing and beheld the shimmering waters of Ravenhurst Lake. The sun's reflection cut a bright path across the ripples made by the wind, and Thomas felt compelled to follow that path with his eyes.

There in the distance, through the trees, he could make out the curved bridge and someone sitting on its railing.

Horror struck his heart as he saw it was Katherine and she was leaning forward as if to jump in.

"Katherine!" he yelled as he ran along the lake's bank, waving his hands, trying to get her attention.

Her head popped up, then she glanced around as if trying to find the source of the noise. Her gaze landed on Thomas as he came barreling out of the trees.

Her surprise over seeing him startled her so much, she began to tip forward. A yelp escaped her throat as she grabbed onto the railing, steadying herself.

Thomas's mind was not thinking rationally, and his first thought was that she was about to throw herself off the bridge. He sped to the bridge, and before she could say anything, he grabbed her waist and pulled her from the bridge. "Don't do it, Katherine," he whispered with great anguish in her ear, holding onto her with her back to his chest. "I could not bear it if you were gone from me."

"Thomas?" he heard her call out softly, and with a smile, he hugged her closer.

"Yes, darling?"

"Let—me—go!" she demanded, putting more emphasis on the last word as she broke his hold on her and whirled around to face him. Thomas was shocked by the anger blazing in her golden eyes.

"Katherine, I've come to tell you—"

"I don't care what you've come to tell me, Thomas. You nearly scared me to death." She pointed jerkily to the railing. "I could have fallen off this bridge!"

"But I—" He stopped when he realized what she'd said. With a questioning frown, he shook his head in confusion. "I thought you were about to throw yourself from it. I came to rescue you!"

Katherine stared at him as if he'd completely lost his mind. "Why would I throw myself off the bridge?"

"Because of how I treated you in town."

She gaped at him. "You think I would kill myself over you?"

Thomas had the grace to blush at such a bold assumption. "Well, I—"

"Thomas, you truly must think I am stupid." She shook her head in disgust. "First of all, I would never think of killing myself over anyone, least of all you. And, second, if I did, it wouldn't be jumping off a bridge into two feet of water," she said, her eyebrows raised and her hands folded over her chest.

Thomas glanced over the railing and, upon seeing the muddy bottom, looked back to Katherine. "Then forgive me, Katherine. I did not stop and think about anything when I saw you leaning over. Especially when I have something of great importance I must speak to you about."

Katherine eyed him with a wary expression. "What could you have to say that you haven't already said?"

Thomas prayed God would help her understand and for-give. "Lucy told me Theodora admitted to your brother she locked you in the room, then sent the servants out of the house so they would not hear you call out," he explained, his voice rushed.

He expected her to be happy he finally believed her. In that moment, he realized his understanding of the female mind was limited.

"I had already told you it was Theodora's fault!" she snapped back.

"But you didn't tell me about the servants," he tried to rea-son. It seemed perfectly logical to him.

"You should have believed me in the first place, Thomas Thornton. Instead, you stood there and peered down your nose at me and passed judgment. I told you I loved you, and you threw it back in my face. *Then* you humiliated me in front of the whole village."

But he stood there and allowed her to voice her anger, knowing he deserved every accusation.

"You are right. I—"

"Do you know how much I have cried?" she continued, ignoring his attempt to talk. She was pacing back and forth on the small bridge. "And now you think I should fall at your feet in gratitude because you have decided to believe me. And not"—she added—"because of anything I have said. Oh, no. But you *do* believe my little sister."

"Katherine, please. Everything you are saying is the truth. But I think I knew all along, in my heart, that you loved me. It was just my pride that held me back."

She whirled around and narrowed her eyes at him. "And where is that famous Thornton pride now? Hmm?"

He held her gaze for a moment, and despite the anger on her face, he could see the hurt and love in her eyes. "My pride is lying at your feet, my beautiful Katherine," he answered her softly. "I know I should have listened and trusted you." He walked closer to her slowly, as one might approach a scared animal. "But if you'll forgive me, I will vow to you, in the presence of God, that I shall trust you with my whole heart from now until I die. I will protect you and never doubt your love for me, my son, or any of the children we will have."

She still was not giving in, but Thomas could see her indecision. "*If* we have children."

"*When* we have children, Katherine." It was a promise. "I want us to marry and start creating our life together as quickly as possible. We have already missed two weeks, you know."

Tears filled her eyes, and he could tell she was fighting her emotions. "I do not know how I should bear it if you did not truly believe I love you. I had set about to do a horrendous deed to you and your family. How can you forgive me?"

Thomas smiled, taking her hands into his own and pulling her closer to him. "As I have studied the Scriptures and realized how Jesus forgives our sins, He expects us to do no less. For me to hang onto my hurt and anger over what you and Theodora had planned would be to rob me of a life of joy with a woman God has put into my life. I believe you when you say you realized you loved me and could not go through with it. But more than that, Katherine," he whispered as he kissed her bare fingers, "I believe that even if you had not loved me, you would not have gone through with it."

Through her tears, Katherine smiled up at him with an expression of relief. "You're right. I felt so convicted from the very beginning. God was trying to talk to me, and finally I broke down and asked for His forgiveness. He truly changed my heart, Thomas. He took away the bitterness I held toward your brother so I could truly love you without any hindrances."

Thomas could hold back no longer. He felt as if a great

load had been taken from his shoulders as he leaned down and pressed a jubilant kiss to her waiting lips. "Will you marry me, Katherine?" he asked.

She nodded as new tears streamed down her rosy cheeks. Only this time they were happy ones. "Yes! Oh, yes, I will marry you!" She threw her arms around him, and he held her tight for a long moment.

Finally he leaned back and said, "Let's do it right now."

She searched his eyes as if trying to gauge his meaning. "Do what right now?"

"Get married!" he exclaimed and laughed when her eyes widened. "The vicar still has the license, and the banns have already been posted. We can marry right now, just the two of us."

She smiled, then seemed to think of something. "We can't marry without Ty! He must be here with us!"

Thomas's grin could not be any larger. "You are right! Let's go to the vicarage and let the vicar send one of his servants for Mrs. Sanborne and Ty."

Katherine tucked herself back into his embrace, laying her head upon his chest. "I cannot wait to be your wife, Lord Thornton."

He kissed the top of her head. "And I cannot wait to call you Lady Thornton!"

She looked up to smile at him but just as abruptly frowned. "Thomas? What happened to your face? Were you in a fight?"

Thomas shook his head. "I was in such a hurry to find you that I'm afraid I met head-on with a tree limb." His smile was self-deprecating as he explained.

Katherine grinned and gently touched his scratched cheek, which had finally stopped bleeding. "You show no scars or signs of wounds from your time spent in the war or during your shipwreck, but now you'll have a tiny scar on your

handsome face, all because you were in a hurry to see me."
She smiled brilliantly at him. "I believe I like the sound of
that. When I tell Lucy, she will declare it your most romantic
gesture to date!"

"I am wounded, and you are pleased about it," he observed,
slightly bemused. "Will I never understand the workings of
the amazing female mind?"

She smiled smugly at him, hugging him once more. "Of
course not, silly. Can any man?"

⊰⊱

Katherine had never felt so loved as she stood beside Thomas
holding the dark pink roses he'd picked for her in the vicar's
garden. Beside them stood Mrs. Sanborne, who, at first, had
tried to hold Ty but finally allowed him to toddle over to his
father, where he clung to his leg, swinging back and forth.

It was a little chaotic, but when Katherine gazed up at
Thomas as he slid the diamond-encrusted family ring on her
finger, she knew she was destined for a wonderful life.

At last the moment came when the vicar announced they
were man and wife. Thomas held her face in his hands and
whispered, "Lady Thornton." He kissed her then, and the
thrill of it made Katherine a little dizzy with excitement. That
quickly turned into embarrassment when the vicar had to clear
his throat in a subtle hint they should bring the kiss to a close.

Katherine was the one who stepped away, but her embarrassment changed to humor when she realized Tyler had been
standing, watching them quietly the whole time. When
Thomas finally looked down at him, he held up his hands as
if to say, "I'm next!" Thomas obliged by lifting his son into
his arms and kissing him soundly on the cheek.

Mrs. Sanborne was the first to speak. "Oh, I don't think I
have ever seen such a stupendous ceremony." She dabbed at
her eyes. "It was stupendously moving."

Katherine and Thomas shared a grin. "You are right on that score, Mrs. Sanborne. It was stupendous."

"Now, to deal with my parents. You do know they will be, and I will use my mother's words, extremely vexed!" Katherine told him as they walked out of the abbey.

"No more so than Nicholas and Christina. I fear we might have to throw a ball or something as a peace offering."

Katherine gazed up into those Thornton blue eyes that were so filled with love and happiness and thought she couldn't possibly be happier. All the hurt and loneliness she'd been through seemed to melt away, and she was left with a hope for the future that seemed so bright and overflowing with promise. A future that included God and a life built on a solid foundation. She would never forget or cease to be thankful God had not only forgiven her misdeeds but had restored to her the only man she had ever loved and allowed her to be a mother to his sweet son.

A smile radiated on their faces as they entered the carriage. Soon they were on their way to Ravenhurst Castle to announce their marriage to her parents.

She hoped her mother had her handkerchief ready.

A Letter To Our Readers

Dear Reader:

In order that we might better contribute to your reading enjoyment, we would appreciate your taking a few minutes to respond to the following questions. We welcome your comments and read each form and letter we receive. When completed, please return to the following:

Fiction Editor
Heartsong Presents
PO Box 719
Uhrichsville, Ohio 44683

1. Did you enjoy reading *The Engagement* by Kimberley Comeaux?
   ❑ Very much! I would like to see more books by this author!
   ❑ Moderately. I would have enjoyed it more if

   _____

   _____

   _____

2. Are you a member of **Heartsong Presents**? ❑ Yes ❑ No
   If no, where did you purchase this book? _____

   _____

3. How would you rate, on a scale from 1 (poor) to 5 (superior), the cover design? _____

4. On a scale from 1 (poor) to 10 (superior), please rate the following elements.

   ____ Heroine   ____ Plot
   ____ Hero   ____ Inspirational theme
   ____ Setting   ____ Secondary characters

5. These characters were special because?_____

_____

_____

6. How has this book inspired your life?_____

_____

_____

7. What settings would you like to see covered in future
   Heartsong Presents books? _____

_____

_____

8. What are some inspirational themes you would like to see
   treated in future books? _____

_____

_____

9. Would you be interested in reading other **Heartsong
   Presents** titles? ❏ Yes ❏ No

10. Please check your age range:
    ❏ Under 18   ❏ 18-24
    ❏ 25-34   ❏ 35-45
    ❏ 46-55   ❏ Over 55

Name_____

Occupation _____

Address _____

City_____ State_____ Zip_____